Snow King
CATCHES HIS
Snowflake

A Three Kings Novel

A.E. VALDEZ

Snow King Catches His Snowflake by A.E. Valdez

www.aevaldez.com

Illustrations by Emily J. Fontana

1st edition 2022

To easy, soft love.

Grab a hot cup of cocoa and your favorite blanket. I hope you have a cozy time in Hope Valley and on Mistletoe Mountain.

This story contains explicit language, vivid descriptions of sex, discussions of death, and mentions of suicide. Please take care of yourself while reading.

1

Noelle

"That's everything," Malcolm says, trying to catch my gaze.

I slide my hands into the back pockets of my jeans, looking around the apartment we've shared for the past three years. The fragments of him, and our relationship, are now packed away in the box he holds in his hands.

"Leave the key."

Setting the box aside, he pulls his keys out of his pocket. "Noelle..." The keys jingle in his hands. "I'm sorry for the way I've treated you."

I laugh dryly. "Malcolm... I'll never forgive you. Not because I hate you, or wish to see you dead, but because you are not deserving of my forgiveness. Are you sorry because of what you did or sorry that I found out?"

"For what I did..." His eyes remain on the keys he has yet to free our – no, *my* – apartment key from.

"Do you know what it's like seeing the person, who you thought was the love of your life, with their tongue down someone else's throat, looking like they're on the verge of fucking in public?"

"I – "

Holding up my hand, I silence him. "If you were tired, bored, or whatever the fuck, you should've used the balls you know how to use so well to fucking tell me you weren't in this with me anymore."

Malcolm could be engulfed in flames right now, and I wouldn't make a move to save him. Three years for what?

"You're right." He hangs his head.

Pinning my arms across my chest, I straighten up. "I know I am. Now if you'll excuse me, I have to get ready for work."

Meeting my gaze, he has hope in his eyes. "You're still going to be my dad's assistant?"

"No," I say flatly. "I handed my notice in the morning after I saw you slobbering on someone else."

I met Malcolm through his father, my former boss. I've been Mr. Pierce's assistant for the past four years. Malcolm came home from college one summer, and I couldn't resist his brown eyes, smooth mahogany skin, and dimpled smile. Should've stayed in my fucking lane. Once he graduated college, he started working with his dad at the realty firm. I'd be an idiot if I continued working at a place where I'd be forced to see Malcolm every day. Mr. Pierce is disappointed to see me go, but also understands I'm doing what's best for me.

"Oh..." He frowns. "My dad didn't say anything."

"He wouldn't have. I asked him not to. Unlike you, he's a man of his word." Malcolm's not used to me being so brazen. Even if I had one fuck left to give in my bucket, it wouldn't be for him. "Look, Malcolm..." I let out an exasperated sigh. "You made your choice, and I'm making mine by choosing me."

Malcolm doesn't say a word as he pulls the key from the ring and sets it on the counter. But of course, he can't go quietly. "I'm sorry things ended like this."

The steel walls I put up around me since his betrayal, soften for a fraction of a second. "Me too."

We were together for three years. I can't pretend that this doesn't hurt like hell, but I'll tend to my wounds in private. He grabs the box, gives me one last look, and heads for the door. I let out a sigh of relief as he leaves, closing the door behind him. Locking it, I let the tears fall.

An hour later, after a good cry, and then getting myself together to make it look like I wasn't crying, I get in my car to head into work. My ringer cuts through my music, alerting me I have a call from sister.

"Hey, Aspen. I'm surprised you're awake." She usually doesn't show any signs of life until noon if she has the day off.

After letting out an unnecessarily loud yawn, she says, "Wanted to check on my big sister."

"I'm fine. I've told you that every day since –"

"And you've been lying every day. It's okay to not be okay, Elle. I hate the asshole too, but that doesn't mean it erases the past three years."

Coming to a stop at a light, I stare at it in silence until it turns green. "Can I tell you something?"

"Tell me your deepest, darkest secrets, my child."

I let out a huff of laughter. "You're so damn dramatic for no reason."

"Spill it. Tell me."

I take a deep breath as I pull into my designated parking space. "Maybe the relationship was over for a while. I felt like... we were going nowhere. But every time that thought crept in, I ignored it. Three years and he showed zero interest in actually getting married, even though he constantly said he wanted to marry me. I wasn't gunning for it or anything, but damn... being on the other side helps me see things through a new lens."

I hear her clapping her hands. "Oh, thank the Gods we're having a radical honesty moment. Noelle, I don't think Malcolm was ever into you the same way you were into him." Her words sting, but I know they're true. "He was too into himself to ever truly appreciate you."

Banging my head against the seat, I ask, "Why didn't you say this before I spent three years hung up on him?"

"You weren't ready to hear it. Now I can, and will, talk all my shit."

I snort with laughter. "Are we going out tonight? Eve wants to come if we are." Eve is my best friend. I met her when I moved here to Hope Valley.

"Hell yeah! You need a good time and maybe even some good dick."

"Bye, Aspen!" She cackles. "Love you."

"Love you too. I'll bring something for you to wear, since you have nothing but office attire."

"It's not that – " I look at my cardigan " – I'll see you tonight."

"That's what I thought," she says smugly.

Cupping my breasts, I argue with Aspen and Eve. "It's barely covering my nipples! You can see my fucking areola!"

Eve falls back onto the bed, laughing. "It'll be dark. You'll be fine!"

"It's not even that serious," Aspen says, standing back, tilting her head side to side. "Just don't... bounce."

"Or fucking breathe! Give me something else. You two have me out here looking like I'm the cousin of fucking desperate." They both double over with laughter. "Sure is funny when it's not your titties on full display."

Eve hands me a different top. "This one is sexy, without looking desperate."

Pulling it on, I'm pleased to see it gives me a respectable amount of cleavage while still leaving a hint to the imagination. "This'll do. Didn't think it'd be my own sister trying to whore me out."

"Hey! I'm just trying to help you in your sugar mama era."

"Shut up." Laughter tumbles from my lips. "It's a decent severance package. Not the lottery."

"It's the least they can do since his worthless son cost you your job," Eve says, looking into the mirror as she touches up her makeup. Her hair is currently a deep burgundy color that's in shoulder length, loose waves. She's wearing a mint colored, corset style top with baggy mom jeans and heels.

"He didn't cost me my job." I roll my eyes. "I *chose* to quit."

I think Mr. Pierce felt bad and chose to put me out of my misery. Towards the end of the workday, he called me into his office to tell me I didn't have to finish out the rest of my two weeks if I didn't want to. I also wasn't expecting a severance package. I'm good with my finances and saving money which is why I chose to quit in the first place. The severance package allows me to breathe without feeling like I have to find a job within the next few weeks. Even though I probably will. Sitting in silence in an apartment I used to share with Malcolm isn't exactly how I want to spend my days.

"You should go on a vacation." Aspen slides into her mini skirt. She's pairing it with a sheer blue, long sleeve top that laces up in the front. "Get out of town." Zipping up her skirt, she fixes her curly, asymmetrical pixie cut. If Tinkerbell was Black and human, she'd be Aspen.

"I can't."

"Why not?" Eve puts the cap back onto her lipstick.

"It's the holidays. You know I love Christmas. I don't want to leave you two alone."

Aspen scoffs. "Sweetie, we don't need you as badly as you think we do."

Gasping, I clutch my chest. "Excuse the fuck outta me!"

Eve scrunches up her face, tilting her head side to side. "Aspen has a point. It's *your* favorite holiday, you should go somewhere you can have fun and unwind. We'll be alright, won't we Aspen?"

"Sure will. You have zero responsibilities besides yourself, take advantage before you jump into the next thing."

I haven't really done anything by myself for the past three years. Malcolm and I did pretty much everything together. Except cheat. "Yeah... maybe I will."

Turning my attention to the mirror, I smile at myself. The bustier top Eve gave me hugs my waist and breast, accentuating my natural curves, with a pair of high-waisted leggings, and heels that will probably be killing me by the end of the night.

"Are you two ready to go?"

"Yes," they say in unison. "Let's go."

A few shots of tequila and margaritas later, I'm feeling lighter when we return to the table after dancing our asses off. I needed a night out at Fireside. It's the best bar in Hope Valley and gets packed on the weekend. I dab the sweat from my forehead, careful not to smudge my makeup.

"I need water. Do you two want anything?"

"Waters," they both say, fanning themselves.

"Got it. I'll be right back." I pull my braids up into a ponytail, letting the cool air kiss my skin. Leaning against the bar, I wait on the bar tender to finish her order.

"Come here often?" a deep voice asks.

I roll my eyes, not even attempting to hide my annoyance. "It's not the '80's, please come up with a better pick up line."

His laugh causes me to look at him. He's handsome with white teeth that look like they're glowing against his dark brown skin. "I still got your attention."

I can't help the smile that tugs at my lips. Choosing to ignore his statement, I order three bottles of water and wait for them. "It may have but – "

Out of the corner of my eye, I see a familiar face. My breath gets caught in my throat as I lock eyes with Malcolm.

"Uh... are you okay?" the man with the pretty smile asks.

"Yeah... " I push my ponytail off my shoulder, tearing my gaze away from Malcolm. The man makes a show of turning around, looking directly at him. "Stop it!" I hiss, swatting his arm. I don't know this man, but I don't want him drawing any more of Malcolm's attention.

He chuckles. "Let me guess, an ex-love interest."

"Yes... is it that obvious?"

"With the way his eyes are boring into my soul? Yeah."

I can't help the laugh that escapes me. "We just broke up. He was cheating. This city is too fucking small." I slap my hand over my mouth, knowing I've shared far too much with a stranger.

"Cheating?" He glances at him again and then back at me. "On you?" His eyes slowly rake over my body. I fidget under his gaze, wondering how long it's going to take to get the fucking waters? "Do you... want to show him what he'll never get a taste of again?"

Raising a brow, I tilt my head to the side, and ask, "What do you mean?"

"Come here..." He gently grabs my wrist, pulling me closer, until I'm standing between his thighs. I nervously glance at Malcolm. His eyes are glued to us. "Don't focus on him. He doesn't matter anymore, remember?"

I nod my head, turning my attention back to his smile, but then notice his lips. They look kissable. As if he reads my mind, his hand comes around the back of my neck, pulling me toward him until I'm a breath away from his lips.

"I'm going to kiss you now, okay?"

I lick my lips in anticipation. "Okay..." I whisper.

"Make it fucking believable," he mutters, pressing his lips to mine.

I freeze momentarily, but relax just as quickly. I thought it'd be a quick peck, but before I know it, our tongues are touching. I don't feel any magic, but I can't deny this man knows how to kiss. My heart jumps in my chest when one of the bottles of water slips from the bar tender's hand, crashing onto the bar.

"That's my water..." Pulling away from him, I clear my throat.

The man glances to his right. I follow his gaze, forgetting Malcolm was even there. Judging by the look on his face, he's seething. Satisfaction warms me. Kissing someone else was... liberating.

"Um... thank you." I grab the waters.

"Anytime." He places his hand over his heart, bowing slightly. "Enjoy the rest of your night."

I stare at him for a moment before beelining back to the table.

"What took you so long?" Aspen grabs a bottle from my hand.

"Uh... Malcolm was at the bar and some guy kissed me. Or," I press my fingertips to my lips. "I kissed some guy..."

"What?!" They both spring up from their seats, craning their necks as they look at the bar.

I look too, but he's no longer there. "He's... gone."

I look at the dance floor and the tables surrounding it. My eyes land on Malcolm who's now sitting with his friends. He's still staring at me, but thankfully stays in his seat.

"Gone?" Eve twists the top off her water. "Was he sexy?"

"Sexy enough for me to kiss him in front of Malcolm. He had a nice smile and was good kisser."

Aspen wipes her mouth with the back of her hand after guzzling half her water. "That's what I'm fucking talkin' about! Soon enough you'll be bouncing on another man's dick, forgetting all about Malcolm."

I chose the wrong time to take a drink. My nose stings as I laugh at the same time I try to swallow. "Damn you, Aspen!"

"Spoiler alert," Eve announces. "Malcolm looks like he's heading this way."

"No! Please get me the fuck out of here."

"Say no more." Aspen wraps her arms around my shoulders, and Eve stands on my other side as if they're my bodyguards.

Aspen steers us to the crowded dance floor. We're jostled side to side as we make our way to the exit. The music blares and the bass vibrates in my feet, but I still hear Malcolm calling my name. I don't bother looking back as we break into a run after moving through the throng of people. The words of the man at the bar echo in my head. *He doesn't matter anymore, remember?*

Eve and Aspen fell asleep hours ago. I tried, but it evaded me no matter how many glasses of wine I downed. Grabbing my robe, I pull it on, cinching it around my waist, and head out to the living room. Looking through the sheer curtain, I see the sun rising on the horizon. I light a candle, grab my laptop, and settle on the couch. A vacation is more appealing after running into Malcolm last night. This whole city reminds me of him. Until I can create new memories, I'll look into getting away.

After an hour of looking, I let out a sigh. Everything is booked because of the holidays. At this point, I'll go anywhere. I was hoping for somewhere with snow since we don't get much here in Hope Valley. Clicking on a few more links with no luck, I'm about to close my laptop, when an ad pops up for a place called Mistletoe Mountain Resort. The A-frame log cabin catches my eye with its background of snowcapped mountains and glittering blankets of snow. I click on the ad and am taken to the resort's page. The only word that comes to my mind is *breathtaking* as I browse the site. It's an adult only resort with hot springs, sleigh rides, reindeer, and they even have a Christmas ball.

"This place seems too good to be true..." I mutter to myself.

My disbelief doesn't stop me from clicking the reservation link. If they have any cabins available, it'll be a fucking Christmas miracle. This resort looks like it has a waiting list for its waiting list. Christmas falls on a weekend this year, so I select a total of five days surrounding it and click the search button. Watching the loading wheel circle around, I hold my breath. My eyes widen as a cabin appears. I waste no time making a reservation. The last time I checked out this fast was for front row seats to my favorite singer's concert.

I quickly open another tab to check for flights. Maybe my reservation was premature, but I'm going to that resort even if I have to drive there. Not that my little car would make it through heaps of snow, or up a mountainside, but I'd sure fucking try. I don't even bat a lash at the insane holiday ticket prices.

"Thank you, Pierce Realty for my nice severance package." I smile, feeling a little satisfaction that this trip is being funded by Malcolm's family.

It takes me a few minutes to fill out my information and check out. When my ticket is bought, I let out an excited squeal.

Eve appears, rubbing her eyes. "What are you doing up?"

"Couldn't sleep." I snap my laptop closed. "So I booked that vacation. Don't tell Aspen this, but she was right."

She grabs the blanket off the back of the couch and sits beside me. "About what?"

"When she said I should take a vacation because I have zero responsibilities right now."

"Oh." Yawning, she lays her head on my shoulder. "True, but I'll be damned if I tell her ass that."

Clapping my hand over my mouth, I stifle the laughter that bubbles up in my throat. "She's too much even if she is right. But..." I set my laptop on the coffee table. "I've been the other half for so long, I want to know what it's like to just be me. You know?"

"I do." I feel her nod her head against my shoulder. "It's not that you two were enmeshed, but he was someone you counted on... even if he did let you down."

"You're not gonna talk shit like Aspen has been waiting to do?"

"Never. I know what it's like to be on this side of heartbreak."

Eve was in a relationship before I met her. We may be like sisters, but the man who broke her heart is a topic she avoids.

"Tell me more about this vacation you're going on," she says, changing the subject.

"It's an adult only resort that looks like a winter wonderland."

"Adults only?" Sitting up, she looks at me with raised brows. "There better be snow blowing happening on this vacation."

"Snow blowing? What the fuck is snow blowing?"

Eve gives me a mischievous smile, making me fear her answer. "You blow in the snow." She makes a motion like she's jerking a dick in her hands.

My eyes widen. "Eve!"

She nudges me. "Don't act like a fucking saint, Noelle. All I'm saying is, make the vacation worth it."

"By having a dick in my mouth?" I tilt my head to the side, wrinkling my nose.

"Yes, but we have more important matters at hand." She reaches for my laptop.

"Like what?"

"Your wardrobe. Sexy snow vixen is the vibe we're going for." I try to take my laptop away from her. "Don't fight it." She yanks it from my hands, pushing me out of the way. "Thank me when you're snow blowing some sexy man on top of a mountain."

2
SNOW

SETTING THE WEIGHTS ASIDE, I wipe my face with a towel, collapsing onto the workout bench. After catching my breath, I grab my phone and head into the sauna. The heat seeps into my muscles before I unlock my phone.

"Call my brothers," I command.

"Calling brothers," an automated female voice responds.

Seconds later, I'm connected to a video call with my two brothers. North answers first.

"I'll be at your place in an hour," he says, pulling a t-shirt over his head.

Winter, as always, answers last. "Morning." He smiles, followed by the sound of a woman giggling in the background. "Aye, watch your teeth, now." She appears in the camera seconds later, laying on his chest. She doesn't have a chance to get comfortable as he sits upright, pushing her off him.

"We've told your dumbass countless times to not answer the phone while fucking," North says, disgusted.

I choose to ignore Winter's guest. "Are you coming to the meeting or are you... preoccupied?"

"She's leaving right now. You know I'd never miss a meeting."

"Good." I nod. "North will be here within the hour. If you're not here by then, consider yourself cut out of the deal." Winter can be erratic with others, but I don't let that shit slide with me.

Winter's cocky smile fades. "I'll be there, Snow."

I nod, ending the video call. Closing my eyes, I sit in the sauna until I have to head up to my room to shower and get ready.

North arrives early. When I enter the kitchen, he's sitting at the table eating breakfast. Looking up, he gives me a bright smile. It always reminds me of our dad. He resembles him the most, but we all have similar facial features. We have deep sepia skin tones, dark brown eyes, full lips, with strong, sharp jaw lines, and black kinky coils. Our frames are similar since we all got into working out – tall, sturdy, and muscular. North looks like the baby, despite the mural of tattoos covering his skin, because he has minimal facial hair while Winter and I have beards.

"Did you come early to eat up my food?" I playfully punch his arm.

"No." He swallows, adjusting his glasses. "Vera insisted."

"Don't put me in the middle." Vera, my chef, holds up her hands in defense. She comes a few times a week to make meals. Somehow, North always comes by on those days. "He was giving me sad puppy dog eyes like I owed him something."

"That sounds more like it." I chuckle, taking my seat at the table.

"What would you like this morning, Snow?" Vera asks.

Glancing at my watch, Winter has five minutes to be here before I keep my word. "Just a smoothie. Thank you, Vera."

When she disappears into the kitchen, North asks, "Will you really cut him out?"

Before I can respond, Winter appears, being escorted by another housekeeper.

"Guess we'll never know."

From the outside looking in, no one would be able to tell Winter is our big brother. The oldest of us three. When our father passed, I bore the weight of our family's legacy on my shoulders. North wasn't ready and Winter wasn't in the right state of mind. If I hadn't stepped up, we would've lost everything and the life we knew. There's a small bit of resentment I have toward him on my part. While he became unhinged, I had to hold it together for the family. I wish I had the freedom Winter has, but at the same time I know he's lost.

"Sorry I'm late." He doesn't follow up with an excuse, knowing I won't deem whatever he says as adequate.

Vera reappears with my smoothie. "Good Morning, Winter. Can I get you anything?"

"I'll take a smoothie and whatever North just demolished, please."

Bringing the glass to my lips, I gulp half of it down. "Neither of you eat at your houses?"

They both smile. "You have better food," North says.

After Vera serves Winter, I waste no time getting down to business. "As both of you know, after fifteen years, North Star Toys is going private. Dad initially made the company public because he wanted to expand across the country and dream beyond the small store he started with mom. When I took over, I learned we were not the majority shareholders of the company like I had initially thought. But as of last week, between the three of us, we now hold the majority of shares. North Star Toys is now ours again."

Winter looks down at his hands before meeting my gaze. His eyes are glossy. "Dad would be so fucking proud of you."

"Of us," I reassure him. Being annoyed with Winter the majority of the time doesn't mean I don't love him.

North clears his throat, drawing our attention. He's the youngest, but the brightest of us three. He's our accountant. Without him, we wouldn't have been able to own North Star Toys again.

"I wanted to wait until we were together to tell you that this holiday season has been our most lucrative yet. Winter creating and managing a social media account has increased sales and allowed us to reach new audiences."

"It's a small contribution," Winter says.

"Don't downplay your wins." I finish the rest of my smoothie.

"Yeah, there's nothing to downplay about us becoming billionaires this year." North gives us a bright smile. "Merry Fucking Christmas, boys."

I choke on my smoothie and Winter, who was leaning back on the chair's legs, topples backwards. North cracks up.

"What?" I say, trying to catch my breath after my coughing fit.

"Yeah, what?" Winter says from the floor.

"It's astonishing to me that neither of you know exactly how much money we have."

"That's what we have you and your nerd brain for." Winter sets himself and the chair upright.

"Yeah, but if something were to ever happen to me – "

"Don't talk like that, North." I cut him off.

He lets out an exasperated sigh, letting his head fall back. "It's a reality that I'm not going to ignore. You two need to be informed. I refuse for us to be blindsided again if something were to happen to one of us."

"He's right," Winter says quietly.

I know North is right, but I don't want to imagine what my life would be like without them. "What do you suggest then?"

"Since neither of you two idiots knew we're billionaires," he says without a flinch as we both glare at him, "both of you need to sit in on the financial meetings even if you don't understand all the jargon. I'll guide you through it. It's easy once you understand it."

"Okay." Winter nods. "That's relatively painless."

They both look at me. I may be the middle child, but I'm the one who makes the decisions. "Alright, we can schedule one for the new year."

North gives me a satisfied smile. "Are you going to be home for Christmas?"

"No. You know I don't celebrate that bullshit." Instead of staying home, I take a vacation somewhere to be the recluse I wish I could be all year round. It's nearly impossible to avoid Christmas all together, but I like to spend it alone.

"President of North Star Toys and you hate Christmas," Winter jokes. "Where will you be this year?"

I shrug. "I don't know. I'll have to ask Wilder what he booked for me." Wilder has been my assistant since I took over for dad. "What about you two?"

"We'll be with mom at her beach house. You should come with us."

After dad died, it took mom a while to figure out what she wanted to do. Eventually she decided to move out of Hope Valley to somewhere that's warm three hundred and sixty-five days of the year with an ocean front view. I'm grateful she's found her peace.

"Maybe next year." I rise from my seat. "I've got to get ready to go into the office. Once you two are done eating all my food, clean up so Vera doesn't have to."

"Aye, aye, Captain," North salutes.

I'll be grateful when our offices close in a few days for the week of Christmas. The weeks leading up to it are hectic. Every year, for the past ten years, around this time I consider saying fuck it all and quitting. Just when I think I can't handle the pressure, it lets up, and I disappear for a week.

"I haven't seen any vacation details for Christmas. Did you make them?" I ask Wilder, stopping by his desk.

"Yes, weeks ago. The details should be sitting in your email." Wilder types away on his computer. "Maybe you should try checking it every once in a while." He smirks.

"Isn't that part of your job?" I ask, sitting on the seat in front of his desk.

"Am I supposed to wipe your ass for you too?" He looks at me over the rim of his glasses.

"I can manage that." I grin.

"It's a Christmas fucking miracle," he mutters. Turning around, he grabs the papers the printer just spit out. "Flight details, rental details, and whatever else you could possibly need. I'll also text you a link with all of this in case you lose the papers."

I take them from his hand, looking them over. "For fuck's sake, could you have picked anywhere more festive? It looks like I'm going to be at Santa's workshop."

"It's a world renowned resort. You're welcome." He smirks.

Flipping through the pages, once I get past the ridiculous Christmas décor, it is a beautiful place. Normally I go somewhere tropical, but this year I wanted to go somewhere with snow.

"That remains to be seen."

"Does it?" He gives me a bored expression. "Why don't you see your way out of the office?"

This is why Wilder is my assistant. He never backs down and keeps my head on straight.

"What are you doing for Christmas?"

"My girlfriend and I are going to my parent's house. I would ask what you're doing, but you'll be playing grinch on the side of a mountain."

My phone rings, cutting through our conversation. Looking at the screen, it's a picture of me with Winter, North, and our mom.

"The way I like it." I flash him a smile, rising from my seat. "Gotta take this. It's my mom. Have a good night."

"Tell her I said hello. Have a good night, Snow."

Swiping the green button to the right, I answer the call. "Hey, Mom. Wilder says hello."

"Hi, Snow. Oh, he's the sweetest." I roll my eyes as Wilder snickers behind me. Grabbing my stuff I head for the elevator. "How are you surviving these days?" I hear the smile in her voice. She remembers the stress my dad experienced in the months and weeks leading up to Christmas all too well.

"Still breathing." I chuckle. "Looking forward to the time off. How are you?"

"Disappointed."

We've done this back and forth for the past five years. "Mom..." I let out an exasperated sigh as I slide into the front seat of my Aston Martin

DBX. Closing the door, I rest my head against the seat, waiting for the call to connect to Bluetooth. "We've been over this. I don't want to celebrate Christmas."

"Snow, this is no way to live your life. Kenna wouldn't have wanted you – "

"Is this conversation necessary every year?"

"Is it necessary for you to avoid your family every year? It was your father's favorite holiday. May I please ask you a question?"

Pinching the bridge of my nose, I say, "Sure."

"Do you think this is how Kenna would've wanted you to continue life?"

A silence follows as the negative emotions grip me. "No..." My voice is barely a whisper.

"You are not responsible for what happened, Snow."

I want to believe her words, but I can't. "I'm going to head home. I love you, Mom."

"Snow..." She hesitates before letting out a sigh, and says, "I love you too."

It's the same nightmare. The one where I'm holding her in my arms, screaming for someone to help us. My mind continuously conjures up this moment, reminding me I didn't save her. No matter how hard I try to wake myself up, I'm stuck reliving this. We had a million unforgettable, good memories, but this is the one I subconsciously choose to play on repeat.

But this time, it's different. Instead of her eyes becoming vacant with her last breath, it morphs from the scene on the road to blankets of snow. When I look down at her in my arms, she's no longer there. I frantically search for her. Whipping around, she stands before me. I almost don't recognize her. I've become used to how she looked in the final moments with blood soaked clothes and the side of her face marred. Her smooth brown skin is now blemish free. She's not glowing with a halo on her head, but she's whole, wearing the dress we buried her in. Her curly hair is shoulder length, like it always was, and I can see the warmth in her brown eyes.

My heart races. "Kenna?" I feel like I can't breathe. Maybe I'll die in my sleep tonight.

"Snow." She smiles, holding her hand out to me.

Cautiously, I reach for it. When our fingertips touch, I pull her toward me, wrapping her in my arms. "You're... here?" I feel the sting of tears in my eyes.

"I'm always here, Snow." She pulls away, placing her hand over my heart.

The realization settles in that this *is* a dream. "That's not enough..."

"Listen to me." She places her hand on my cheek. I'm surprised by its warmth. I lean into it. "You need to let me go. Our time together was short, but I need you to live. Not just exist."

"You don't know what you're asking of me." I look away from her.

"I do." She catches my gaze, giving me a captivating smile. "I'm tired of watching you punish yourself day in and day out. And to be honest, it's quite boring."

Despite the emotional pain that's gripping me, I laugh. Kenna always knew how to turn a shitty moment into an unforgettable one. She was the color to my world. "It's not the same without you."

"You wouldn't know because you're too busy paying penance you gave yourself," she quips. "I don't blame you for what happened, Snow."

I've seen her every night in my dreams since the night of the accident five years ago. This is the first time she's spoken to me. Maybe I'm insane for the sense of relief that washes over me, knowing she's not real and this is all in my head. But I can't help but be grateful to hear those words coming from her lips. Even if it is a figment of my imagination.

She swipes a tear from my cheek. "There's enough room in that heart of yours to love again. Remember, love heals just as much as it breaks."

"I love – " Before I can finish my sentence, she begins to fade along with the scene around us. "Kenna?" I try to hold onto her hand, but it slips through my fingers as she disappears.

"Time to start living again, Snow," her voice echoes.

The scene of us on the road reappears, and she's back in my arms with a vacant stare. This time, I don't rewatch. I wake up, bolting upright, untangling myself from my sheets as I wrench them off me. I'm drenched in a cold sweat, and the cool air hitting my skin sends a chill through me. Hunching forward, I rest my elbows on my thighs, trying to catch my breath, and calm my racing heart.

"What the fuck…" I mutter, rubbing my eyes.

I've really gone off the rails if I'm having conversations with my dead fiancée in my dreams. Once my heart stops hammering against my chest, I glance at the clock on my dresser and let out a sigh when I see it's just past three in the morning. There's no way in hell I'm going back to sleep.

Rising to my feet, I grab a pair of sweats and pull them on. I head out to my living room, turn on the fireplace, and pour myself some whiskey.

I sink into the overstuffed chair that sits in front of the fireplace and wrap a quilt my mom made around my shoulders. As I tip my glass back, my eyes are drawn to a picture that has the flames flickering across the glass. It's my last photo with Kenna taken on Christmas morning. Getting up, I grab it from the shelf and sprawl out in the chair again. Holding the glass of whiskey to my temple, I stare at us suspended in a perfect moment. I'd just proposed, and we'd spent the entire day celebrating our engagement and Christmas with her family.

It had all shattered that night on our drive home. One second we were planning our future together and the next our car hit a patch of black ice, spinning us out of control. Kenna was ejected out of the car when we started to roll. She didn't have her seatbelt on, and I didn't notice to remind her. I was too caught up in the fact that she was going to be my wife. Maybe if I had noticed, she *would* be my wife right now. Logically I know the accident wasn't my fault, but I haven't allowed myself to accept that.

I'm not sure I can accept a reality without her in it. A smile tugs at my lips as our conversation replays in my head. It would be like her to call my life boring. She didn't have to tell me that the way I've been living isn't what she would want for me. I haven't dated anyone since her, but that hasn't stopped my family and friends from trying to set me up. The few dates I have been on never result past anything but sex because I don't allow them to. There also hasn't been anyone I'd care to explore more with.

Looking at the photo for a few more minutes, I rise to my feet and finish off my glass of whiskey before setting it aside. I give the picture one last glance before placing it back on the shelf, wondering if I'll ever feel alive again without her.

3.
Noelle

AT THE ENCOURAGEMENT OF Eve and Aspen, I'm at the spa getting buffed and polished before leaving for my vacation tomorrow.

"You two realize this trip is for *me*, right?" I grab an ox blood red from the nail polish selection. "Not my vagina."

"Oh, please." Aspen scoffs. "Just because your love life has died doesn't mean your vagina has to suffer."

My eyes widen, hoping no one hears my loudmouth sister as I look over my shoulder. Eve falls into a fit of laughter at the mortified look on my face.

"I've been single for a two and a half weeks. You make it seem like I'm on my way to a nunnery."

"No, but you were with Malcolm for three years, having shitty sex no doubt." Eve flanks her arm over my shoulders. " It's time for you to taste the rainbow." She whispers the last part as if she's a spokesperson for Skittles.

"First of all," I narrow my eyes, shrugging out of her hold, and they swallow their laughter. "I appreciate you two trying to liberate my yoni, but she's fine. We're fucking fine. I just want to go and enjoy some goddamn solitude. I was with someone for three years. Can I please, *please* just do this for myself?"

Having them hover over me since the breakup has been suffocating. I appreciate that they care and are here for me, but they're not helping me by thinking fucking someone else is going to resolve my issues. I'll still miss Malcolm, Hope Valley will still remind me of him, and I'll still fucking care about him for only heaven knows how long. I've accepted this is where I'm at. They haven't.

"I'm sorry, Elle." Aspen swallows, clearing her throat. "I just... want you to feel better."

"I know, and I love you for that." I give her a small smile. "But I need space to feel the way I feel for however long I want to feel it. I'm not going off the deep end, guys. I'm just trying to process."

Eve pulls us into a group hug. "We got your back. Always."

"One thing I'll always know is that with you two I'm never alone."

The energy lightens as I hug them back. Thankfully, the conversation steers away from my love life and toward nail polish colors. I'm debating on what color I should get my toes painted when my phone starts to vibrate in my bag. Pulling it out, my lips turn up in a smile when I see it's my dad.

"Hey, Dad." I answer, smiling at the screen.

"Hi, honey. Aspen told us about you and Malcolm. How are you holding up?" If looks could kill, Aspen would be dead where she stands. She cringes and waves in my direction. Our mom appears on the screen. "If you need anything at all, let us know."

"Oh, I will." I force a smile while yelling at Aspen with my eyes.

"She also told us that you're going on a vacation. We think it's good to get back out there." My mom smiles as dad nods his head reassuringly.

"Wow. Is there anything Aspen didn't tell you?"

"Sorry," my sister mouths.

"Aspen was worried is all. When do you leave for your vacation?"

"Tomorrow. We're actually about to get our nails done." Eve and Aspen wave at the camera.

"So happy to see you have support with you."

The nail tech lets us know they're ready. "They're supportive alright. Mom, Dad they just called us back. Can we call you later?"

"Yes, of course. Love you two. And you too, Eve."

Eve smiles and waves goodbye. Aspen and I say our goodbyes before I hang up the phone.

"You know what I find funny?" I glare at Aspen. "That I have yet to utter a single word about you dropping out of nursing school, but they know my entire life story."

"Elle – "

I place my finger over my lips, making a shushing noise. "Remember that the next time you're worried."

She nods, clamping her mouth shut. Eve looks at her, shaking her head as she laughs.

Our parents had us much later in life than they had anticipated. Mom didn't think she could have kids. Then at thirty-eight years old, she got pregnant with me. Two years later, Aspen was born. They're both retired, traveling the world now. We spend every other Christmas with them, and then see each other throughout the year. This year I gave up going to see them to spend Christmas with Malcolm's family. Aspen decided to stay here in Hope Valley for the holidays and join me. But Malcolm ruined those plans. Aspen didn't want to bother with trying to find a last minute flight to be with our parents in Egypt, so she's spending it with Eve and her family instead.

I quickly grab a white polish off the shelf for my toes and join the girls in the massage chairs for our pedicures.

Eve was staying with me tonight to take me to the airport in the morning, but I think she could tell I needed space. She made up some excuse about a deadline she forgot about for work. I give her a tight squeeze before heading up to my apartment. The nice thing about Eve and Aspen being with me so much the past week is that the apartment now feels like *mine*. They went with me to the home decorating stores and encouraged my retail therapy. I was worried the apartment would always feel a little empty without Malcolm. Instead, I'm in love with it all over again and enjoying my solitude.

My phone vibrates with a text from Malcolm as if my thoughts called to him.

Malcolm: Hey. Did I leave my razor there?

This is his segue into talking to me? A razor? The same razor I saw in the box he took with him when he moved out. I'm actually surprised I didn't hear from him sooner, considering he was so desperate to talk to me at Fireside the other night.

Noelle: No.

Best to keep it short.

Malcolm: Are you busy tonight?
Noelle: Yep.
Malcolm: Oh.

I set my phone aside and resume packing, but my phone cuts through my thoughts again.

Malcolm: How have you been doing?
Noelle: Just fine without you.

Staring at the screen, I furrow my brow. Was this what I was enamored with all these years? The bare fucking minimum? No. Not even that. He dug so far below the bar, he's delusional enough to think he still has a chance. I'd be lying if I said I hadn't thought about getting back with him, but it's nothing my vibrator can't fix. It's not like he was providing me with toe curling sex or even emotional support for that matter. My self-respect won't allow me to entertain his texts. I leave him on read when he texts me back.

A few hours later, I finish packing. The girls helped me purchase a new wardrobe. My clothes weren't as "boring" as they made them out to seem, but I did need to refresh my closet. Most the clothes I had were bought with Malcolm in mind. But after seeing how the woman he was tonguing down looked, I realized I probably have never been his type. I'm the type his parents approve of. Someone who would look good on his arm and in photos which is probably why we were together for so long.

After taking a shower, I go through my after-bath ritual of moisturizing my body and applying skin care products. Then I put on my bonnet and climb into bed. Butterflies of excitement dance in my stomach, anticipating jetting off to a winter wonderland mountain resort.

Eve pulls up to the drop off lane at the airport. The sun hasn't even risen yet. Putting the car in park, she reaches behind her and sets a bag in my lap. I give her and the bag a curious look. When I go to open it, she places her hands over mine.

"Look, I know you're not planning on meeting anyone. But if the opportunity presents itself, I don't want you to have a reason to not take it."

Raising a brow, I open the bag and peer inside. When I see what it is, I cover my face, laughing. "Really, Eve? How could I possibly need a box this big?"

I pull out the industrial size box of condoms, and she beams at me.

"Hypothermia is real, Noelle. You'll need to stay warm somehow." She shrugs her shoulder, giving me a sly smile.

Putting my hand over my mouth, my shoulders shake with laughter as I stare at the box. "Thank you for always looking out for me."

"Of course. Just because you have them doesn't mean you have to use them. Above all, enjoy yourself. You deserve it."

I don't say anything as I wrap her into a tight hug. "Love you."

"Love you, too." She unwraps my arms from around her. "Now, go. Have fun."

I give her one last smile before I climb out of the car, grabbing my bags and head inside to check in. Hastily, I shove the bag containing the rubbers into my carry on. When I reach security, I think nothing of it until I have to set my bag down for it to be inspected. My face immediately heats, making my neck itch as I helplessly watch it get closer to the TSA agent. Wiping my sweaty palms on my jeans, I try not to look nervous as I step through the metal detectors. I should've put them in my suitcase. At least then I wouldn't have to look at someone.

I feel a small bit of relief when my bag goes through the scanning box and slides to the end of the line. As I get ready to grab it, a TSA agent reaches it before I do. Of course it's a man and of course he's handsome.

"Morning, Ma'am." He nods. "Need to take a closer look at an item in your bag."

My breath gets caught in my throat. All I can do is smile at him, hoping I don't look constipated and suspicious. He's tall with deep brown skin and muscles that look like they refuse to be confined by his uniform. What is it about men in uniform? I snap out of my thoughts when I hear the rustling of the bag. I pull my bottom lip between my teeth, biting down on it. He looks at the box of condoms before quickly glancing at me. His eyes flit from the box to me a few more times, and I give him a big smile while dying inside.

He shoves the bag and box back into my bag, handing it to me. "I hope you have an... enjoyable vacation. Happy holidays."

"Uh... thanks." I snatch my bag from his hands nearly forgetting my shoes, and other items. Turning my back to him, I grab my things and beeline it for the gate. My nerves calm once I'm a fair distance away from security. What the hell was I thinking putting that box of rubbers in my bag? Oh well, it'll be a funny story to tell the girls once I'm back.

An hour and a half later, I board my flight and I'm grateful no one is sitting beside me. Resting my head against the window, I settle in for the six hour flight.

Mistletoe Mountain feels like an entirely other world. Pictures couldn't even capture the true beauty of this place. Glittering blankets of snow stretch for miles, meeting a dense forest of pine trees that climb to the top of the snowcapped mountain. Nestled in the line of trees are A–frame style cabins that look like they were designed to fit the environment instead of disrupting it. I'm so mesmerized by the stunning views that I bump into someone.

"Excuse me." I smile apologetically after brushing shoulders with a woman.

Nodding, she smiles and continues on her way. My distraction continues as I step into the receptionist area. A fire is blazing in a fireplace so large that I could probably walk upright inside of it. Twinkling lights and garland with red berries and pine leaves wrap around the large wood columns in the lobby. There is a giant Christmas tree beside the fireplace expertly decorated with the most intricate ornaments. Tearing my eyes away from the exquisite views and décor, I focus on checking in.

"Enjoy your stay, Miss Frost. You're in cabin six." He hands me a key that's dangling off a keyring with a gold bell. "Your bags are already there. Will you need help getting to your cabin? It's about a five minute walk from here."

"No. I think I can manage. Thank you." I take the key from him.

"Of course. If you need anything during your stay, my name is Nicholas."

I nod, giving him a smile and sling my bag over my shoulder. Heading outside, I inhale the crisp, refreshing air. There's a path to the left that leads toward the market area that looks like a Christmas village. I can't wait to explore the shops once I get settled in the cabin. Walking the path toward the cabins, I wish I would've made a longer reservation because I don't think five days is going to be enough. Sliding my phone out of my back pocket, I snap a few pictures to send off to my parents, Aspen, and Eve to let them know I made it safely.

The path to the cabins steadily inclines, making me winded, and I feel a trickle of sweat down my back. I can't wait to take a steaming hot shower and sit in front of the fireplace. The cabins seem close together from afar, but there's enough distance between them that they feel secluded. Finally, I reach cabin six.

Opening the front door, I let out an audible gasp. The back of the cabin has floor-to-ceiling windows that face the pine trees with a view of the mountain behind it. There's a tall Christmas tree that nearly reaches the exposed beams and skylights of the ceiling. I run my hand along the buttery soft dark brown leather couches in the living room, sinking my fingers into the fur blankets draped over the back of them. There's a kitchenette with a table tucked into the corner.

Walking down the hall toward the bedroom, I'm pleased to see it has the same windows and view as the living room. The bed has plush pillows and blankets, making me want to dive into them, but first, I need a shower after a six hour flight and the trek up the hill. Pulling at the zipper on my jacket, I strip out of my clothes and head for the bathroom. It also has a large window that's facing a more heavily wooded area. It looks like a mirror window. I can see out, but if someone were on the other side, they couldn't see me with my ass out. There's a waterfall style shower with glass doors. I walk right past it to the giant tub. Turning the water on I let the tub fill up while I strip out of the rest of my clothes.

All I need is a glass of wine. I reach for a robe, then shake my head, remembering I'm alone and can walk around naked if I damn well please. Pouring myself a glass from the complimentary bottle of wine, I return to the bathroom where the tub is almost full and steam is rising from it. I set my glass of wine on the tray lying across the tub, tie up my braids, and sink into the warmth.

Taking a small sip of wine, I relax and enjoy the views. Finally, some peace.

4
SNOW

I TRY NOT TO roll my eyes too hard at the overwhelming Christmas décor scattered around the lobby when I arrive. To appease my annoyance, I send a text to Wilder.

> **Snow: You did this on purpose, didn't you?**
> **Wilder: I'll do what I want when your fate is in my hands.**
> **Snow: And I'm the grinch?**
> **Wilder: You're the only person I know who is threatened by a good time.**

I audibly scoff even though he can't hear me.

> **Snow: I am not.**
> **Wilder: Are too.**
> **Snow: Am not.**
> **Wilder: Are too.**
> **Snow: I enjoy a good time.**
> **Wilder: When is the last time you had one?**

Staring at my phone, the realization sets in that I can't remember the last time I *truly* enjoyed myself. You'd think becoming a billionaire would do it, for most it would, but for me it's just another pinnacle of success. I prefer to be alone and–fuck... I really am boring.

Wilder: Damn. Having to dig into childhood memories huh?
Snow: No. I don't have time to entertain you while checking in.
Wilder: I have zero expectations considering you can't entertain yourself. Thank me when you get back. Merry Christmas, Snow.

Chuckling, I decide I better actually check in instead of going back and forth with him.

Snow: Merry Christmas.

I shove my phone into the front pocket of my jeans and check in. Instead of getting a ride to the cabin, I walk. I flew in on a private jet, but I still get restless after being up in the air for hours at a time. I need to stretch my legs and breathe fresh air. While walking, I take in the views. The blankets of snow remind me of Kenna's dream. I don't know if it means anything. Maybe something good will happen while I'm here. I chuckle at myself for daring to believe something good would happen to me.

Dad would've loved this place. Kenna too. Dad passed ten years ago and Kenna passed five years later. Over the last decade, I've learned to avoid things that are painful reminders of what I've lost. And apparently, that's fucking everything. My best friends are my brothers. We've been that way since we were kids. Wilder is the closest thing I have to a friend,

SNOW KING CATCHES HIS SNOWFLAKE

and we've never even been out to drinks or anything else together. When those I loved ceased to exist, so did I.

Stepping into the cabin, I'm grateful the Christmas décor isn't as gaudy as it was in the lobby. The only thing Christmassy is the tree in the corner near the fireplace. Setting the keys on the counter, I shrug out of my hoodie. As I'm pulling it over my head, an ear piercing scream fills the air.

"Fuck!" I shout, getting tangled in the sleeves as I try to cover my ears and take it off at the same time.

When I finally wrench it over head, my eyes land on a woman with a towel tightly wrapped around her and braids that reach her waist. Her eyes are wide with fear as she backs up, toppling over the ottoman. The towel that was around her falls to the floor, and I try to cover my eyes while simultaneously trying to help her up. She scrambles backward away from me, and somehow, she's still fucking screaming. I'm surprised the windows haven't shattered with her pitch. She frantically reaches around until her hands land on a bag. Spilling the contents on the floor she lunges for a glittery red can.

She bolts upright, pointing the can at me. Holding my hands up, I don't have enough time to react before she's spraying me with fucking pepper spray.

"Get out!" she screams shrilly.

I let out a growl, placing my hands over my eyes, that silences her screams as the pepper spray takes effect. In my effort to get the hell away from her, I trip over the ottoman she just tripped over. She gasps when my head hits the floor with a thud.

"Are – Are you… okay?" For the way she was just screaming bloody murder, I'm surprised she's soft spoken. I feel her hand touch my arm, and I nudge her away from me.

"Am I okay?" I ask through gritted teeth, writhing around on the floor, coughing and feeling like I can't breathe. "You just assaulted me with pepper spray, causing me to hit my head on the floor. What the fuck do you think?" I can't see her face yet because my eyes feel hotter than the pits of hell.

"Who are you, and why the hell are you in my cabin?" she demands.

"Your cabin?" I let out an involuntary groan from the pain. This woman really wants to have a conversation now? It feels like someone is stabbing my eyes with needles. I attempt to open my eyes to glare at her, but immediately shut them again.

"Yes. *Mine.* Why are you here? Are you some… voyeur?"

"I should be asking you the same damn question. Did my brothers hire you?" My head begins to throb.

"For what?" she asks, her tone dripping with incredulity.

"I don't know." I shrug, trying to refrain from rubbing my eyes. "You're naked… in my cabin, so I thought – " The sting of the slap that follows is heightened by the pepper spray. "Fuck!" I shout. "What in the actual fuck is wrong with you?" I'm going to fucking kill Wilder.

"Me? What the fuck is wrong with me? You just called me a–a… prostitute." She whispers the word, and it makes me chuckle despite the urge to toss her, ass naked, into a snow drift.

"There is nothing wrong with sex work," she continues, "but for that to be your immediate presumption is bold."

"You called me a voyeur," I retort.

"Yeah, well you try coming out of a relaxing bath to a giant standing in the living room."

"A giant? What the hell does that mean?"

"All I saw was a big, tall guy dressed in all black, taking his clothes off. You'd spray yourself with pepper spray too."

When she puts it that way, she's right. Instead of admitting that, I ask, "Why are you in my cabin?"

"It's not yours." I hear the frustration in her voice. "You probably got the wrong cabin number or something. This is cabin– "

"Six. I don't make mistakes." I attempt to open my eyes again with no luck. "Listen, as painful as this conversation has been, unless you're going to help me, call the front desk. I don't give a fuck whose cabin it is."

She has the unmitigated gall to let out a long low sigh as if I'm the fucking problem. "Fine."

I feel her hand wrap around my wrist. "What are you doing?" I ask, pulling away from her.

"Do you want help or not?"

To my annoyance, I blindly follow her lead. The burn of the pepper spray is still at molten lava levels. I squint through my eyes every few steps, but I can't really make out anything. She could be leading me outside for all I know. Wouldn't put it past her. She slips her hand into mine, pulling me forward.

I hear her turn on water, grabbing my hands, she places them under the cool stream.

"Rinse your eyes and face. I'm going to grab some soap."

I begin rinsing my eyes. It doesn't wash away the burn, but it dulls it. I feel her hand on mine again as she squeezes something into my hand.

"Use this to wash and keep rinsing your eyes out." I hesitate, pausing with my hands under the water. "It's just dish soap. Goodness."

"Oh, excuse me for being skeptical of you."

"Yeah, yeah. I'll be back."

After rinsing for what feels like an eternity, I'm finally able to open my eyes. Looking at myself in the mirror, I'm relieved that I can see, and there's no visible damage other than redness. The woman responsible for my current state of affairs meets my gaze in the mirror. She has large, almond shaped deep brown eyes that I don't want to look away from. I also take note that she's now fully clothed, wearing a red top that sets off her lustrous umber skin tone. She sucks her plush bottom lip between her teeth, biting on it. To my surprise, my dick betrays me, and twitches in response.

Her gaze doesn't waver from mine as I scowl at her. Instead, she fucking smiles, and for a fraction of a second, I feel like I'm standing in the sun. My scowl deepens.

"Um..." She licks her lips, clasping her hands tightly in front of her and bounces on the balls of her feet. "Hi. I'm Noelle."

I raise a speculative brow. "You just pepper sprayed me and instead of apologizing, you introduce yourself?"

She slides her hands into her back pockets, shrugging. "You see... in order for there to be an apology... I have to be sorry and I'm not."

I straighten up to my full height, crossing my arms, and tilt my head to the side. I didn't think I could be anymore vexed, but the woman standing before me is smiling beside the definition. "You're not?"

"No. Well, I didn't mean for you to hit your head. But you ran into that ottoman and timberrrrr..." She makes a motion with her arm, imitating something falling, followed by a crashing sound. I continue staring at her, trying to make sense of why she's here. "How is your head? I have Tylenol if–"

"I want to figure out how to get you out of my cabin because your presence is doing nothing for my headache."

"It's not your –" She throws her hands up, rolling her eyes. "I'll call reception. You're going to feel dumb when they tell you to pack your shit and get out."

"No. We're going over there so I can warn them that you're assaulting people with pepper spray."

"I am not! You're an intruder."

I ignore her and walk out to the living room. Grabbing my suitcase, I head toward the bedroom. She's on my heels the entire time.

"What do you think you're doing?" She watches me.

Opening my suitcase, I grab a pepper spray free t-shirt, and my jacket. Ignoring her concerns, I pull them on. Without a word, I tear out of the front door and head toward the office. Seconds later, I hear running footsteps, and unfortunately, the source of my problems appears beside me, zipping up her jacket.

"This wouldn't have happened if – "

"You hadn't pepper sprayed me," I finish the sentence.

"What else was I supposed to do? I had no fucking clue as to who you were, and I still don't." She jogs beside me in her ridiculous Moon Boots, attempting to keep up with my long strides. It makes me smile, internally.

"That's the least of my worries at the moment. We'll get this sorted and go our separate ways."

"If anything," she continues. I look up at the sky, wondering what I did to land myself in this cluster fuck. "You should be apologizing to me, don't you think? I mean you were–"

Slowly turning my head to the side, I glower at her. She catches the vibe, closing her mouth and focusing on the path ahead. We continue in silence, but I feel her eyes on me every few seconds.

"You know," she says, shattering the brief silence. "Your brows are perfect for the whole pensive stare thing."

I brush my hand across my brow line, wondering how my brows can be perfect for a pensive gaze. "Do you always talk this much?"

"Do you always talk so little?"

"Yes," I say flatly.

Her momentary silence lets me know she wasn't expecting such a blunt response. I talk when I feel comfortable, and she is definitely not someone I associate with comfort. A sense of relief washes over me as the lobby comes into view. Instead of talking, she's resorted to humming Christmas songs. I steal a glance at her out of the corner of my eye. Considering what she did to me not too long ago, she's alarmingly beautiful. It's a thought I haven't had in a while. Of course I've been around pretty women, but they all start to blur after a while when their intentions are the same. Noelle catches my gaze, giving me a smile. Instead of returning it, I open the door to the lobby for her.

After explaining the situation to two different employees, one of them finally gets the manager. While we wait, Noelle doesn't miss an opportunity to talk.

"Your name is Snow?" Amusement dances in her eyes.

It's a question I get asked routinely, and the curiosity only grows when they hear my brother's names are North and Winter. Since my dad was a toymaker, my parents took the whole Mr. and Mrs. Claus thing rather seriously. When I was younger, I hated it. Kids can be assholes. But as I've aged, I've learned to appreciate the uniqueness of it.

"Yes, and if you're going to make a bad joke, I've heard them all." I look around, hoping they're able to find the manager. If not, I will.

"I wasn't actually." I meet her gaze, surprised. "It's a nice name." She smiles.

This time I let the corner of my mouth tip up before turning to see the manager appearing. He's speaking in hushed tones to the employee who was doing a shit job of helping us.

"Hello. My name is Nicholas."

"Hi, Nicholas." Noelle waves with a smile. I give her a curious look. "What? We met earlier."

Tearing my gaze from hers, I return my attention to Nicholas. "Are you going to explain to us why we're sharing the same cabin?"

He adjusts his glasses, frowning at the computer. "Unfortunately, we double booked cabin six…"

"Double booked?" I try to keep my voice level. "How? Are you using pen and paper for your bookings?"

"No, Sir. There can be discrepancies between booking through our website and using a third-party agency. It's supposed to automatically update the system, and it didn't. I can see that you booked in November, and Miss Frost," he smiles at her, making me annoyed, "booked last week. When my associate checked you in earlier, she assumed you two were together." His eyes flit between me and Noelle.

"*Together*?" I give him an incredulous look. "This woman pepper sprayed me. We are far from together, and I would like to be even further apart."

"You deserved it." She chimes in.

Ignoring her, I ask, "Is there an extra cabin?"

He cringes. "Unfortunately, due to the holidays, everything is booked."

"Of fucking course it is. You know– " I stop abruptly when I feel a hand on my arm, looking down I realize it belongs to Noelle.

"It's fine, Snow." Her voice caresses my name. "I'll just... figure something out." I stare at her for longer than I should. "What? If I'm able to pepper spray you, I think I should be fine."

Snapping out of the trance hearing my name on her lips had me under, I say, "No. You shouldn't have to figure it out because our friend Nicholas here," I glance at him. "Is going to figure out some way to make it right, won't you?" I'm smiling, but there's nothing friendly about the look on my face.

"I–I most certainly will," he stutters.

"Good. We'll– " When I turn to look at Noelle, she's already out the door, walking down the path to the cabin "I'll be back for you, Nicholas." I point at him.

He swallows, nodding. I run out the door after Noelle.

"Hey," I say, catching up to her. "Where are you going?"

"To get my stuff," she says without a glance in my direction.

"No. They can– "

"Snow..." Stopping in her tracks, she closes her eyes, and takes a deep breath. Fixing me with her gaze, she says, "I've dealt with a lot of bullshit lately. I came here for peace, and it's been anything but that. If I'm lucky, I can find a flight back home before Christmas."

"What?" The woman who pepper sprayed me and the woman standing in front of me seem like two entirely different people.

"I'm tired." Her shoulders sag. "I don't want to argue. A few hours ago, my biggest concern was where I'm going to take a nap. You clearly booked the cabin first and – "

"We can share it," I say, against my better judgement. "The cabin..."

"Huh?" She gapes at me. "Not even five minutes ago you wanted to be as far away from me as– "

"For clarity, I still do. But then I saw you moping your way back to the cabin."

"I'm not moping" She straightens up, glaring at me. "Look, Snow. I'm sure deep... deep... deeeeep... buried – "

"Get on with it, Noelle." I motion my hand for her to wrap up her monologue.

"Deep, deep, down," she continues, "you're an amazing human being, but you don't *really* want to share a cabin with me. You're acting like I'm the bane of your existence when it's clear you were miserable long before we crossed paths."

"The fuck?" I cock my head to the side. "Miserable? You fucking pepper sprayed me! My skin *still* burns, by the way. So, of course I'm going to be miserable."

"It was an accident, okay? You terrified me. I thought I was alone and – "

"I'm sorry I..." Straightening up, I clear my throat and grumble the rest. "For scaring you..." My dad raised me to be a respectable gentleman. If that were me, woman or man, I would've done much worse than pepper spray them.

"What?" She stops mid-rant.

I narrow my eyes, knowing she heard me good and damn well. "I said... I'm sorry for scaring you."

Looking up at me, a smile appears on her lips. "I'll stay. Can I have the bed?"

This is where my respectability stops. "No." I don't spare her a glance as I head back toward the cabin.

5
Noelle

Brooding.

That's the word I'd use to describe Snow. I give up on trying to keep up with his long, determined strides and fall into my own pace, walking behind him. He's wearing a black jacket, slim fitting black jeans, and black boots. Earlier, when he changed his shirt, not only did I light up like a Christmas tree at the sight of his lean, muscular build, but I also noticed he packed lots of black and a few neutrals. About as exciting as his personality.

Snow is handsome, striking, and every other synonym for those words. He clearly works out and takes care of himself. Even with a full, neatly trimmed jet black beard, the angles of his face are sharp. His hair is cut low, but not too low, with faded sides. I'm still able to appreciate the way his kinky coils shine in the sun. He has a single gold necklace with a medallion on that glints against his rich sepia skin. I'm so lost in thought, I run into his brick wall of a back.

Holding my nose, I look up at him. "What the hell?"

His eyes remind me of obsidian pools with the faintest twinkle in them. "I asked if you had the key?"

"Yes." I nudge past him, rubbing my nose, and open the door. "For you being so sure it was your cabin, I'm surprised you didn't have your key," I say, shutting the door behind us.

"If I sprayed you with pepper spray, you'd want to get the fuck away from me too," he says over his shoulder, disappearing down the hall.

Seconds later, I hear the shower and I try to think about anything other than him being naked. I can't deny that I'm physically attracted to him despite his unsavory attitude. And perhaps I have a screw loose because that makes him more attractive. Rummaging around the kitchen, I look for stuff to make hot cocoa. After opening a few cabinets, I find a kettle and grab the small tin of hot cocoa from the welcome basket.

Putting the water on to boil, I debate on asking Snow if he'd like some, even though that man probably wants nothing from me. I don't know what I'm thinking, staying in this cabin alone with him. He's made it abundantly clear that he doesn't want to be around me. But then why offer to share the cabin? Maybe he'll be more pleasant when the effects, and the memory, of the pepper spray wear off.

A knock at the door interrupts my thoughts. Hopefully, it's not another person saying this is their cabin. At least I'm fully clothed this time. Opening the door, I'm met by the manager.

"Hi, Nicholas." I step aside, waving him in.

"Miss Frost." He smiles.

"Let me go get Snow. He's cleaning up since I pepper sprayed him."

"Oh." His eyes widen in surprise. "I thought he was being... dramatic earlier when he said that."

"It was indeed a recollection of true events. I'll be right back."

The bedroom door is ajar, and I poke my head in cautiously. "Snow? Nicholas is here." I wait a few breaths for a response before entering.

As I near the bathroom, I close my eyes because I don't know if he's decent. The smell of him surrounds me and I inhale deep. Of course he smells good. I pick up a subtle note of bergamot, refreshing and clean. Whatever he uses, I don't mind being wrapped up in it.

"Why are your eyes closed?"

I jump at the smoky timbre of his voice. "Because," I keep them closed. "You were showering, and I didn't want to impose."

"You can open them."

I let my eyes flutter open and have to keep the look of shock off my face when I'm met by his chest. Sure I saw it earlier, but now if I were to lean forward I could lick the droplet of water trailing over his pec. My eyes briefly flit down his abs, counting eight of them and notice he has a towel slung low, very low, on his hips. I meant for it to be a quick glance, but it takes me longer than necessary to tear my eyes away from his pleasure trail. Raking my eyes back up his body, I notice a few tattoos embellishing his skin. Tipping my head back, I look up at him, meeting his gaze.

I notice there's a ghost of a smirk on his full lips. "Um... you have nice lashes." Wait... what? Nice lashes? I mean the man does have some nice lashes, but why the fuck of all the things to–

"You came in here to tell me I have nice lashes?"

"No. I..." Why the fuck did I come in here? My eyes dip back down to his chest before recalling, "Nicholas is here. The manager. He wanted to speak with you. Us." There's a stray droplet of water dangling off his beard. Before I can think of what I'm doing, I swipe it away. He doesn't flinch away from my touch like I assumed he would. "There was water... and..." A random thought occurs to me. "How much did you see earlier? When I tripped over the ottoman?"

Tilting his head to the side, he raises a brow. "Enough." Stepping around me, he reaches for his suitcase on the bed.

"What... does that mean exactly?" My voice rises an octave.

"It means," he says, pulling a pair of boxers out of his suitcase. I quickly turn around, giving him privacy. "I saw enough."

"Yeah, but like... *what* did you see?" I don't know why I care. It's already happened. I'm sure he saw everything.

It's silent for a moment, and he appears in front of me again. "What does a towel cover, Noelle?"

My heart races as he holds my gaze, but before I can respond he leaves. I catch my breath before following behind him to talk with Nicholas.

"Mr. – "

"You can call me Snow."

Nicholas nods. "Very well, Snow. I tried to find other accommodations and – "

"She's staying with me." Snow cuts in, finality in his tone.

I'm sure it's not healthy for my heart to be beating the way it is right now. Nicholas looks at me, and I shrug, rubbing my hand across my neck to calm the prickle of nervousness that just crept up it.

"Okay..." Nicholas's eyes bounce between Snow and me. "Your stay this week is complimentary, Snow. Miss Frost, I've refunded your stay as well. The two of you have full access to the spa and your meals will be taken care of by our restaurant, The Ridge. However I do ask, if you are planning to dine at the restaurant that you make reservations. Will you be attending the Christmas ball?"

"Yes," I say enthusiastically while Snow grumbles, "No."

I side eye him. "What?" he asks. "Christmas isn't my thing."

"Okay... Grinch." He glares at me, but I'm getting used to it so I ignore him. Turning my attention back to Nicholas. "That sounds perfect, Nicholas. Thank you."

"Of course, Miss Frost. Do you have something to wear to the ball? If you don't, be sure to check out Mistletoe Square. There is an array of shops there."

"I do." I beam at him. "Are you going to the ball?"

Nicholas seems caught off guard by my question. "Yes, of course."

"Good." I smile. "You'll owe me a dance."

I feel Snow's eyes on me. Nicholas quickly glances at him before saying, "Wouldn't miss it. Snow..." He hesitates. "Are you satisfied with this?"

I turn to look at him. If he isn't satisfied with a free stay and free food this man is a fucking grinch. He holds my gaze for a few breaths, before turning his attention to Nicholas.

"It's up to Noelle." He turns his attention back to me. "Are you happy with this?"

"Uh..." It's my turn to be caught off guard. After being concerned with someone else's happiness for three years, it's nice for someone to ask me this. Even if it's coming from him. "Yes."

"Good." Nicholas visibly relaxes. "Please don't hesitate to call if you need anything."

Snow sees him out the door at the same time the kettle begins to whistle. Removing it from the stove, I grab the tin of hot cocoa. I see Snow out of the corner of my eye as I reach for a mug. He surprises me by taking a seat at the kitchen island, watching me. Why am I suddenly so interesting? For the first time since we met, he's not glaring at me, and for some reason I find it more unsettling.

Breaking the silence, I ask, "Did you want some?"

"Yes, I'll take some. Thank you." I blink in confusion. Was he just... nice to me? "What?" he asks.

"Nothing. You just surprised me by being nice..."

He lets out a hearty chuckle. "I've calmed down."

I grab another mug. "So you're not always so... formidable?"

"Depends on who you ask. Are you scared of me?" He licks his lips.

"No," I say without hesitation. "I know you mean me no harm."

"Good." His shoulders relax a little. "Although I have to disappoint you and tell you I am not a voyeur."

I smirk. "If you enjoy watching other people, who am I to judge?" Truth be told, I'd love to watch him. I can only imagine what the rest of him looks like. My cheeks heat with embarrassment. Thankfully my melanin keeps him from seeing the blush.

"It depends on the situation." He says casually, holding my gaze.

I look away from him, focusing on measuring out the hot chocolate. "How did you end up on Mistletoe Mountain if Christmas isn't your thing?"

"My assistant, Wilder, who loves to be a pain in my ass, made the reservation."

"Do they still have a job?" I raise a brow, concerned.

He gives me a genuine smile. "He's been with me the past ten years."

"I'm impressed." I slide a cup of cocoa toward him. "Here I was thinking four years at my last job was a lot."

"What happened?"

"Um..." I look into my cup of cocoa. "You don't want to hear my sob story."

"How do you know?"

SNOW KING CATCHES HIS SNOWFLAKE

I chew on the inside of my cheek. "Alright," I say, figuring I have nothing to lose. "But I want to enjoy my cocoa in front of the fire."

He follows me to the living room, and we sink into the chairs near the warm flames. I tell him everything about Malcolm and me. How we met, fell in love, and broke up. "I feel more hurt than anything." A tear makes its way down my cheek. "Looking back now, we weren't really going anywhere. We were just comfortable."

The night everything unraveled, I sobbed. No matter how disconnected we were, the emotional pain was relentless.

"Clearly," I flinch when his thumb touches my cheek, but I relax into his touch as he swipes it away. "He was way too fucking comfortable." I laugh softly at his comment. "How did you see him cheating? Did someone tell you or... ?"

"He sent a text meant for her to me. It was a restaurant with a time. I thought we were going on a date... until I saw them."

Snow finishes his cup of cocoa, setting it on the coffee table. "You may be hurt, but would you rather be hurt and alone or alone with someone who doesn't give a fuck about you?"

I'd be a fool to claim Malcolm cared. He only cared after the fact. "Alone and hurt."

"Is that why you're here?"

"Yeah. My best friend and sister have been staying with me consistently since the breakup. I love that they care, but I need room to breathe."

"I know that feeling all too well." He rests his head against the chair.

"Why is Christmas not your thing?"

His body goes rigid. I'd think something was wrong with him if it weren't for the controlled rise and fall of his chest.

"I'd rather not talk about it."

"Shit, I'm sorry. I didn't – "

He abruptly rises to his feet. "I'm going to the bar."

"Oh... okay." He sets off for the front door, grabbing his jacket from the hook near it. "Do you want some company?"

He pauses with his hand on the door. "No."

I watch him step out into the night and make his way toward the lobby. I thought we were finally getting along. Maybe staying here with him was a bad idea.

6
SNOW

THOUGHTS OF KENNA SWIM in my head while I down glass after glass of alcohol. I didn't need Noelle to mention Christmas for me to think of her. She hasn't left my mind since the dream I had last week. It's not that I never talk about her, I'm still in touch with her family, but it's painful to trudge into the past even though I seem to be stuck there. A woman, wearing too much perfume, sits beside me.

"Can I buy you a drink?" she asks, attempting to make her voice sound smooth when she's two sheets to the wind.

"No." I don't spare her a glance as I signal the bartender for another glass of whiskey.

"Oh, C'mon. I'll make it worth your while." She tries to trail her fingertips up my arm.

"I highly doubt it will be," I say, moving away from her touch. "There's a room full of people, find someone else to regret in the morning."

"Fuck you, asshole." She sneers, getting up from her seat with a huff.

"Cheers." I tip my glass toward her as she stumbles away.

"Didn't think you'd still be pissing off women," a familiar voice says behind me.

Recognizing the voice, I turn toward it. "Brielle?"

"How are you?" She wraps me in a hug.

"I'm doing alright. Are you here with Ezra?" I look around for her husband.

"I am, but I took his ass back to the cabin after he fell off the barstool."

I chuckle, shaking my head. "Still doesn't know how to hold his liquor?"

"Nope." She shrugs with a smirk. "His phone fell out of his pocket when he took a tumble. I'm hoping the bartender has it. Mind if I have a drink with you?"

"I'd love that." I smile at her.

Brielle gets the bartender's attention. Relief washes over her when they hand her Ezra's phone. She orders a drink, and we fall into easy conversation, catching up on what we've been up to since we last saw each other. Brielle was best friends with Kenna and still lives next door to her parents.

"I just know your father is proud of you and your brothers. How's your mom?"

"Thank you. My mom is good. I'll be seeing her soon."

"Tell her I said 'hi' when you do." She smiles, taking a sip of her drink. "Are you here with someone?"

"Me?" I ask as if it's the most asinine thing ever uttered.

I see the twinkle of amusement in her eyes. "How crazy of me to think you'd ever allow yourself to be happy again." Brielle has never tried to set me up, but whenever we have run into each other, she never misses a chance to give me shit. "I'm not telling you how to heal, but you know Kenna is probably talking so much trash about you wherever she is, right?"

I chuckle into my glass as the dream replays in my head. "Wouldn't doubt it." Even in life, Kenna always encouraged me to be happy. "You'll revel in the fact that I am unintentionally here with someone then."

She signals the bartender for another drink, leaning closer to me. "Unintentionally? Pray tell."

I tell her about my literal run in with Noelle and the mix up with the cabin reservation. She cackles about the fact she pepper sprayed me. "I haven't decided whether I like her or not yet."

"You must if she pepper sprayed you and you still offered to share the cabin with her."

I order a water from the bartender. "She was... moping. Where else was she going to go?"

"Home. Like she said." She stirs her drink. "Is she pretty?"

"Brielle..."

"Snow, answer the fucking question. I'll be the bitch and say it – " I try to interrupt her, but she presses on. "Kenna isn't coming back, and you're not going to find her in someone else."

Brielle is the only person I allow to talk to me about Kenna in this way. Losing Kenna hurt her just as much as it hurt me. They knew each other since they were kids. If anyone loved and knew Kenna as much as I did, it was Brielle.

Brielle watches me expectantly, and I look into my glass as I say, "She's insufferably gorgeous."

She smiles, looking pleased with herself. "Why isn't she here at the bar with you?"

"I – she asked why Christmas isn't my thing, and I froze up." After I got to the bar, I felt like an ass for the way I left her there. She tells me about her relationship with her boyfriend and then I go cold.

Brielle places her hand on my shoulder. "Things hurt a little less the more you talk about them."

I know she's right. Brielle was the one who put me in touch with a therapist after we lost Kenna. "Yeah… but I don't know her."

She lifts a shoulder, stabbing at the lemon in her drink. "Maybe that's what you need. Someone who doesn't share the past with you so you can only look forward to the future."

I nod my head slowly, letting her words sink in. Ezra's phone lights up with a picture of Brielle.

"I know his drunk ass is not calling me from my phone right now." Rolling her eyes with a huff, she silences it, turning her attention back to me. "We should get together for dinner. Bring your roommate." She stands, finishing off her drink.

"Uh… Brielle, I don't – "

"Snow, honestly, what do you have to lose?" She sweeps her locs over her shoulder. When I remain silent, she says, "Exactly. You don't have shit to lose."

"Okay…" My voice is laced with uncertainty. "Text me a time."

"I will." She smiles, giving me another hug. "I'm so happy I ran into you tonight."

Without another glance, she leaves me at the bar. Kenna may not be here physically, but lately, I can feel her everywhere.

Arriving at the cabin, I remove my jacket. Noelle is lying on the couch with her legs slung over the back of it. She has her headphones on and a book in her hands. Hopefully, she doesn't assault me again. I stop in the kitchen for more water. When I look at her, her eyes are on me. She looks away quickly, focusing on her book. Letting out a sigh, I head to the bedroom to change my clothes and also to figure out how to talk to her.

We'll be spending the next five days in close proximity. I'd prefer for them to not be awkward. Pulling on a hoodie and some sweats, I return to the living room. She still has her headphones on with the book in her hands. Sitting near the fire, I decide to wait until she's done with her book. I'm not sure she's reading with the way she's stealing glances at me. After a minute of this, she slides her headphones off, looping them around her neck.

"You glare a lot. Did you know that?"

"I'm not glaring." I slip my hands into the front pocket of my hoodie.

"So that's just your natural state of being?"

"No... this is my face." I chuckle. "I'm not doing anything."

"Ah... I see." She nods. "You also suffer from RBF. Welcome to the community."

Shifting in my seat to get a better look at her, I ask, "Suffer from what?"

"RBF. Resting bitch face."

"Bitch face?"

"Oh, c'mon. I know you've seen the memes online." Shaking my head no, she continues. "It means you look annoyed even when you're resting. Get it?"

The term makes me chuckle. "Yeah, I do."

"How old are you?"

"Are you calling me old?"

She smiles, setting her book aside. "No. I'm curious."

"Thirty-three."

There are a few breaths of silence before she speaks again. "You're not going to ask me my age?"

"My mom taught me it isn't polite."

"That's fair. Good to know you're a gentleman."

We hold each other's gaze. "So... how old are you then?"

Smiling, she says, "Thirty. I'll be thirty-one in February."

"A few more months." I knew she had to be at least twenty-one to rent a room, but I'm relieved that she's closer to my age.

She gets up from the couch, walking to the kitchen. Grabbing the bottle of wine from the welcome basket, she holds it up. "Want some?"

"No. I'm good. Thank you."

I watch her grab a glass, pour some wine, look at it, and then pour some more. The corners of my mouth turn up. Bending over, she looks in the fridge. I shouldn't stare, but I do anyway until she turns around, holding a charcuterie board. She rejoins me in front of the fire.

"Were the drinks good at the bar?" She grabs a piece of cheese and a cracker, putting them in her mouth.

"I wouldn't know. I don't get mixed drinks. The whiskey was good."

"I'll have to go before I leave."

"I'm sorry for the way I left earlier."

She waves her hand, dismissing my apology. "You're not obligated to tell me anything you don't want to."

Before I can talk myself out of it, I say, "I lost someone I love on Christmas day."

"Oh..." She sets her glass of wine aside, giving me her full attention. "I truly mean this," she says, placing her hand over her heart. "I'm sorry for your loss." There's nothing but sincerity in her eyes and warmth in her voice. "May I ask who were they to you?"

I had only meant to apologize for earlier, not tell her my life's story. "She was my fiancée."

I tell her about Kenna. How we met, us dating, the proposal, and the night she died. I'd like to blame it on the whiskey, but despite our initial meeting, Noelle makes me comfortable. Perhaps it's the unfamiliarity or the fact I know she cares without having to know her.

I also tell Noelle about the dream. "She basically called me boring..."

"Mmm..." she says, drawing my attention to her as she nods her head. "Mhm, yep. I can see that."

"Wait... what?" I scoff under her scrutinizing gaze. "You barely know my name."

She holds her hands up in defense. "It's the stoic expression, brooding behavior, and the all black wardrobe." She waves her hand down the length of my body. "I mean..." She shrugs as if that sums it up.

"I have endless outfit options with neutral colors."

She lets out a huff of laughter. "Endlessly boring."

"And your Moon Boots are exciting, how?" I tilt my head to the side with the corner of my mouth tipped up.

"Ohhh," she giggles. "Holding that one in all day were you?"

"It's hard not to notice them when you're clomping along beside me."

"They're cute!" she defends.

"By whose standards?" Her laugh is infectious, making me laugh too.

"Mine, you ass!" Holding her stomach, she attempts to catch her breath.

For the first time in a long time, I'm enjoying myself. When her laughter dies down, I say, "Thank you for listening."

Before I can register what's happening, she hugs me. I relax into her. I can't remember the last time I had a hug like this. It warms me to my core, radiating through my body.

"Any time." In the silence that follows, her stomach growls.

"Have you... not eaten?" I pull away, looking at her.

"No. I was going to until I got sucked into my book."

"Do you want me to make you something?"

She blinks at me as if my question takes her by surprise. "Make me something?"

"Yeah. I can make a mean grilled cheese," I say, eyeing the French sourdough bread and array of cheeses on the charcuterie board.

"Prove it." She smiles.

We move into the kitchen. She sits on the counter, talking to me, while I make us grilled cheese sandwiches. After meeting her this morning, I couldn't have imagined cooking for her. Let alone talking and laughing with her the way I am right now. The only people I'm around regularly are my brothers, Wilder, and my housekeeper. Noelle is a pleasant change of pace for me.

Opening my eyes, I blink down at Noelle in confusion as she sleeps with her head resting in my lap. We sat on the couch to eat grilled cheese sandwiches, drink wine, and talk last night. Sunlight is streaming through the window now. Its brilliance is enhanced by the snow clinging to the pine trees and blanketing the ground. Rubbing the sleep from my eyes, I gently move Noelle's head off my lap. She stirs momentarily, falling asleep again.

Checking my phone, there's a missed call from every member of my family and text messages. Apparently they don't understand the concept of a vacation. No matter where I go in the world for Christmas, they never fail to check in nearly every hour to make sure I'm doing okay. I call my mom back, because if not she'll worry.

She answers on the second ring. "There you are. I tried reaching you all day yesterday. How's your trip so far?"

"Good." I say, yawning. "I'm going to get ready so I can enjoy my vacation."

"Is it so wrong a mother worries about her son?"

"No, but if I were going to kill myself, Mom, I would've done it a long time ago. Or... there's always tomorrow..."

"Snow!" She reprimands me. "I have no idea where you got your morbid sense of humor from, but I don't find it funny."

I can't help but laugh. "Mom, I'm good. I appreciate that you check on me." Honestly, if she wasn't checking on me, I'd be worried.

My words calm her down. "Alright, I'll let you enjoy the rest of your stay. Love you."

I know she'll call me tomorrow morning too. "Love you too, Mom."

Hanging up the phone, I grab my toiletries bag and head into the bathroom to do my morning routine.

Standing in front of the mirror after my shower, I line up my beard. My phone starts ringing again. Tipping my head back, I let out a sigh. My family wants me to get out. When I do go out, they can't leave me alone. Grabbing my phone from the nightstand, I relax when I see Brielle's name on my screen.

"Hey, Brielle."

"Hey. Do you want to meet around six for dinner at the restaurant near the lobby? Ezra's family will arrive later tonight, and we won't have much time the rest of our trip."

"Yeah, that sounds great."

"Bring your cabin mate."

"Brielle, I don't think that's – "

She lets out an exasperated sigh. "Snow. It's dinner. Not a wedding. What are you going to do? Just tell her you're off to dinner and not invite her? That's rude as fuck. Bring her or don't bother coming."

"Damn. It's like that? You haven't even met her and you're threatening me like this?"

"Everyone else has time for your woe is me dramatics. I don't. See you at six."

I'm met by the beeping noise, letting me know the call ended. Pulling it away from my ear, I mutter, "She really hung up on me..."

I scrub my hands down my face, collapsing back onto the bed. I'm filled with trepidation. The last time I asked a woman to dinner was when I asked Kenna out on our first date. Any dates I've been on the past five years were setup by my family, and I only went to appease them. Why do I keep calling this a date? It's just dinner.

"Rough morning?" Noelle asks from the doorway.

I sit up on the edge of the bed. "No. I was just thinking about something."

"About what?" Gathering her hair, she pulls it into a bun.

"It's fine. Just a call from a friend."

She opens her suitcase, pulling out some clothes and toiletries. "You know what overthinking gives you?"

"What?" I pique a brow.

"Anxiety." She smiles.

I chuckle. "Thank you for that sound advice."

"Are you done in the bathroom?" Her eyes flit down to the towel around my waist.

"Yeah, go ahead."

Once the door closes behind her, I adjust myself. She looked at me the same way yesterday when I got out of the shower. I was grateful that she was too busy talking to notice my reaction to her eyes.

Nearly an hour later, Noelle emerges from the bathroom, and I'm surprised to see she's still not ready.

"Do you want to go to breakfast with me?"

How did she ask me to breakfast so effortlessly and I'm struggling to ask her to dinner. She's looking at me expectantly. "Yeah. Of course. Are you ready... or should I wait another hour?"

"I would've never guessed..." She frees her hair from it's bun, letting her braids fall down her back.

"Guess... what?"

"That you have a sense of humor." She smiles, making her brown eyes light up.

"Damn. I walked right into that one."

"Give me twenty minutes to finish getting ready."

Exactly twenty minutes later, she reappears in what I'm guessing is a snow suit if Catwoman was on a winter vacation. It's molded to her body like it was made for her.

She glances down at her feet, holding her arms out to the side. "What?"

I blink, not realizing I had been staring at her longer than necessary. "Nothing. Decided to give the Moon Boots a rest today, huh?" They've been replaced by black combat boots that hug her calves.

"Oh, fuck you!" She cackles. "Let's go. I'm starving."

I gladly enjoy the view, following behind her.

7
Noelle

I DIDN'T THINK SNOW and I would ever be on speaking terms after the way we met yesterday. Yet here we are, enjoying breakfast together. This morning, I'm seeing him in a different light. The look in his eye that I quickly dubbed as annoyance I now recognize as sadness. A longing for what once was. I couldn't fathom losing someone I love. I've never experienced a loss of that magnitude. Breaking up with Malcolm is the only thing I have to gauge it against, and I don't perceive him as a loss.

After eating a plate of cinnamon brioche French toast skewers, and drinking a few mimosas, we step out into the frosty morning. I pull on my gloves, jacket, and slip on my hat.

"Any plans for today?"

"Yeah." He shoves his hands into his jacket pockets. "But not until later. You?"

"I have a date."

The crease between his brows deepens. "A date? With who?"

"Reindeer," I beam.

He blinks, shaking his head. "What?"

"I have a date to feed the reindeer in..." Pulling up the sleeve of my jacket, I glance at my watch. "An hour. Would you like to join me?"

He gives me a charming smile. "Normally I'd say no to being the third wheel, but I'll join you."

"Perfect." I loop my arm through his, directing us toward the rental area. "You can drive the Go kart." I have yet to see a car around here.

"Go kart? You mean the snowmobile?"

"Yeah. That thing." I stop in my tracks. "That's if you're okay with driving..." I didn't consider he may not even drive now that he lost his fiancée in an accident.

"Thank you for being considerate, but I don't mind driving."

I let out a sigh of relief. "Thank God! Because I've never driven in snow like this before, let alone a Go kart."

"Snowmobile." He lets out a hearty laugh. "Did you invite me to be your chauffer?"

"I invited you because I like having you around... so far." I pull him along beside me.

When we reach the rental office, he pays for the snowmobile rental. The reindeer farm is two and half miles away from the main resort area.

Handing me a helmet and goggles, he asks, "What were you going to do? Walk the whole way in the cold?"

"I was considering it." He tries to hold back a smile. "But you're here so we don't need to talk about that now."

"Are you going to be warm enough in that?" He points to my suit. "I have to stop by the cabin for a heavier jacket and pants."

"You've done this before?"

"Yeah, we used to go skiing every year with my dad before he passed away."

I can't help the tears that well in my eyes. "He passed away?"

"Don't look at me like that," he says.

"Like what?" I sniffle.

"Like *that*." He points at me.

I look up at the sky, trying to blink back the tears. "I'm not looking at you like anything."

"Noelle..." He lets out an exasperated sigh. "I'm fine."

"Fine? You lost your dad." I can't help the tear that escapes. How is he still able to breathe after experiencing that much loss? I steal a glance at him, and he's giving me a look of incredulity. "I'm sorry. I can't help it, okay?"

"Thank you for sympathizing with me, but I'm fine. Can we go on your reindeer date now?"

I wrap my arms around him. He freezes for a few seconds before returning my hug. Pulling away after a few deep breaths, I say, "Alright. I feel better. Let's go feed the reindeer."

He laughs as we climb onto the snowmobile.

I'm glad we went back to the cabin for warmer attire. I didn't think it could be any colder, but even with a thick jacket, woolen socks, boots, and a hat – I still feel the chill in my bones. However, coming to see the reindeer is worth the temporary discomfort. They're magical. Stepping into the enclosure, we're surrounded by the herd.

Holding out my hand, I wait for a reindeer to approach me. I'm like a kid seeing Santa for the first time. One walks toward me, eating from my hand.

"Snow!" I whisper loudly. "Get my phone and take a picture."

"Where is it?" he asks in a normal, outside voice.

"Shhh! You'll scare him." I see the misty cloud of his breath as he sighs. "My phone is in my back pocket."

He slides his warm hand into my pocket, making me momentarily forget I have a reindeer eating from my palm. "How do you even know it's a male?"

Sucking my teeth, I roll my eyes. "Were you not listening to them?" I nod my head toward the owners. "They said males have bigger antlers than females."

"I'm going to be honest, I zoned out."

"Typical man."

"Hey!" he says defensively, but I see the amusement in his eyes. Holding up the camera, he points it at me. "Smile." I give him the cheesiest smile I can muster. He lets out a warm laugh. "That works."

"Let me take a picture of you two," the owner says, holding out her hand for my phone.

He looks between me and her, unsure of what to do. "Be a good sport, Snow. Take a picture with me."

"I don't have any food for the – " Before he can finish his sentence, the owner puts some food into his hand, nudging him toward me.

I bite on my bottom lip to keep from laughing and grab more food. He stands beside me, holding out his hand, and waits for a reindeer to approach him. It takes less than ten seconds. Two reindeer stand in front of us, eating from our palms. He may not admit it, but I see the wonder in his eyes.

I gently bump into his arm. He tears his eyes away from the reindeer, looking down at me. "It's fun huh?"

A smile spreads across his lips. "It is."

"Told ya," I say smugly.

Once the food is gone from his palm, she hands my phone to him. "You two are a cute couple. Enjoy the rest of your day."

"Oh, we're not..." His voice trails off as she walks away.

"I don't think she heard you. Speak up." I snicker.

He steps toward me, making me swallow my laughter as I look up at him. Snow puts his arm around my waist, and I can't help the way my breath hitches. Sliding my phone back into my pocket, he says, "I knew you were a smartass."

Smiling, he turns his back to me and grabs another handful of food. It suddenly doesn't feel so cold with his touch.

Later that afternoon, we return to the cabin. Taking off all my gear, I collapse on the couch in front of the fire. I didn't think visiting the reindeer farm would take most of the day. Closing my eyes, I contemplate going to the restaurant for dinner or ordering in and eating it in the hot tub. The latter sounds very appealing.

Unzipping the top half of my body suit, I open my eyes to see Snow standing in front of me. "Hi. How can I help you?"

His eyes are glued to my exposed piece of skin. "I wanted to ask..." He meets my gaze. "Do you want to – "

"Yes."

"Huh?" he asks.

"The answer is yes."

Crossing his arms, he cocks his head to the side. "You don't even know what I'm going to ask you."

"So what?" I shrug. "You're harmless. If you were going to kill me, it would've already happened."

He nods, chuckling. "That's a fair conclusion."

"What were you going to ask me?"

"To dinner."

"You made it seem like you were going to ask me to jump off a cliff with you."

"No, but..." He looks unsure of himself. I wait for him to continue. "It's with Brielle and her husband."

"Okay... and?"

"She was Kenna's best friend."

Sitting up, I look at him. "Am I missing something here? Are you guys cannibals and I'm the meal or what? Why do you look physically ill?"

"You don't think it's weird... going to dinner with my late fiancée's best friend?"

"Is this a swingers situation?" I narrow my eyes at him. "Because if it is, I have – "

"No. Hell no. That is – " He stops mid-sentence when I fall back onto the couch with laughter. "You really don't care?"

"No, Snow. I don't. I'd love to go if you genuinely want me to be there. The question is, do *you* care?"

"I..." He takes a seat in the chair. "I haven't asked anyone to... anywhere since before Kenna. My family has set me up on dates, but I've – "

"Would you consider me a friend?" My question stops him from spiraling.

"Yeah. I would."

"Then lets go to dinner as friends."

"Okay." He lets out a sigh of relief.

"Your overthinking was giving me fucking anxiety." I stand, stretching. "Have you ever thought of just letting things be what they are instead of labeling it?"

I leave him with his thoughts while I go get ready for our friendly dinner date.

A few hours later, I'm sitting at the table with Snow, Brielle, and Ezra. Snow finally got out of his head and seems to be enjoying himself. Brielle and Ezra are a beautiful couple. She has high cheek bones, brown eyes, smooth ebony skin, and black locs that flow down to her ass. Ezra has a personality that is larger than life, and I'm sure he is the party wherever he goes. He's tall and lean with dark brown eyes, rich mahogany skin, arms covered in tattoos, and he has loose curly hair that frames his face.

We ate a nice dinner, and now we're talking over drinks and dessert.

"Where are you from, Noelle?" Brielle asks, taking a bite of her chocolate mousse cake.

"Hope Valley." She looks between Snow and me, eyes wide with surprise. "Did I miss something?" I take a bite of my peppermint cheesecake.

"You live in Hope Valley?" Snow gapes at me.

"Yes. Why is this shocking?"

"I live there too," he says and I give him the same shocked look he just gave me.

"Have you been giving her the cold shoulder this whole time?" Brielle asks Snow with a smirk.

"No," he says defensively. "We had breakfast this morning and spent the afternoon feeding reindeer. Where we live hasn't come up in conversation until now."

"Look at you, socializing," Ezra says with a grin. "Bout fucking time. You two will have to link up when you get back."

I wait for Snow to panic and refuse, surprisingly he doesn't. He's still looking at me as if I was hiding that I live in Hope Valley from him.

"Better yet," Brielle smiles. "The four of us should. We live just outside of Hope Valley."

"Bronze Hills?" I ask. It's still considered part of Hope Valley, but it's a smaller suburb area.

"Yep. Born and raised," Ezra says proudly.

"Small world." I smile. Looking at Snow, his eyes are still on mine. "Don't look at me like that." I imitate his tone from earlier today. He smiles, looking into his glass before tipping it back.

"Where do you work, Noelle?" Brielle asks.

"Uh... I'm in between jobs right now, figuring things out." I'd prefer not to dive into that subject, so I redirect the conversation back to them. "What about you guys?"

"We own Fireside. Have you been?"

"What?!" I exclaim. "Of course I've been. Who in Hope Valley hasn't been there yet?" They both give Snow an accusatory glare. I side eye him. "How is this possible?"

"It's not my scene." He shrugs casually.

"All I'm hearing is 'I'm boring and can't support my friends.'" I mimic his tone.

"I mean... I didn't want to say it," Ezra says.

"Oh, I like her." Brielle laughs.

"I'm busy," Snow says defensively.

"Doing what?" I lean toward him. "Brooding?" Ezra and Brielle stifle their laughter.

Snow gives me a look of indignation. "I don't – you're making me sound like a fucking recluse."

"If we're being honest..." Brielle shrugs her shoulders. "Sounds spot on to me."

"Prove me wrong." I turn my body to face him with a challenging smirk on my lips. "When was the last time you willingly went out because you wanted to?"

"I thought I talked a lot of shit." Ezra looks at me with admiration.

"Nah, I think she has you beat," Brielle says.

"Today. With you. When we went to feed the reindeer." I can't mask the look of shock on my face. Snow leans back in his chair. Reaching his hand out, he places his fingertips underneath my chin, gently closing my mouth I didn't realize was open.

"Silence, Noelle?" He smirks, rubbing his thumb against my chin before putting his hand back in his lap.

The gesture creates a pool between my thighs. Brielle says something, but I don't hear her because I'm too busy staring at Snow. I was talking all that shit to Aspen and Eve that this trip was for me and not my vagina, but here I am wondering if he'd like the taste of me sitting on his face.

Snow nudges my leg with his. "What?" I ask, looking around the table.

"Ezra was talking about the brewery they're opening up, and Brielle wanted to know if you'd like to attend the family and friends opening." I see the amusement dancing in his eyes.

"Yeah." I look at Brielle, smiling as if I wasn't just having dirty thoughts.

"Perfect." She doesn't miss a beat, sliding her phone toward me. "Give me your number."

Ezra's phone chimes with a text. "Babe, the fam just touched down."

I hand Brielle her phone. "I'll text you. I'm happy we got to have dinner together. Ezra's family is here, and we're going to meet them back at the chateau. We came a few days early to enjoy ourselves and unwind before all the Christmas festivities."

"It was a pleasure meeting you guys." I smile. "Enjoy the time with your family."

Rising from our seats, Brielle and Ezra pull me into hugs as if they've known me their whole lives.

"We better see more of you, Snow," Ezra warns.

"I don't know that Noelle will allow me to miss anything."

Smiling, I say, "I'll drag him along behind me, kicking and screaming."

We say our goodbyes, walking out of the restaurant, and go our separate ways.

Snow surprises me, draping his arm over my shoulders. "Thank you for joining me tonight, friend."

I laugh softly. "It was fun. They're really nice people." The snow crunches beneath our feet as we walk back to the cabin.

"They are." He smiles. "But you were right."

"About what?"

"I need to show up for them more. They were the only two people to meet me where I was at after Kenna died. I felt like everyone else was trying to push me out of grief... make me feel better... but they just let me be while also letting me know I wasn't alone."

It reminds me of Aspen always trying to make everything better. "Are you showing up for yourself?"

"Nah," He answers honestly. "Not for a while."

"It's hard to show up for people when we can't see ourselves unless we're standing in front of a mirror. Give yourself grace. They'll be there for you no matter what."

I look up at the stars bathing in the moonlight as we walk. When I look at Snow, his eyes are on me.

"I'm happy I met you, Noelle."

There I go melting into a puddle again.

8
Noelle

SNOW IS LYING ON the giant California king sized bed when I get out of the bathroom. This cabin was clearly designed for couples, not strangers. Although, I'd like to think we're a little more than strangers now. It's interesting how you meet someone and click. Well... we didn't click initially, but we're getting along well now. I enjoyed hanging out with his friends. To be honest, I was worried it was going to be awkward. Neither Brielle nor Ezra were going to allow me to feel uncomfortable. I'm glad I went with the flow and joined them.

I spent my soak in the tub trying to decide if I should sleep in the bed with Snow. He's sprawled out, and even his large frame looks normal in the bed. It's big enough we won't even touch. We slept together last night on the couch. I don't know why he'd be reluctant now.

"Snow."

"Hm..." Looking up from his phone, his eyes linger a little longer on my exposed thighs.

"We're friends, right?"

"Yeah," he says without hesitation.

"Okay." I smile.

He gives me a look of confusion before I leave the room to grab my pillow and blanket. I climb onto the bed, making myself comfortable.

Once I find a spot to sink into, I look at him. His eyes are on me, and I grin.

"The couch is nice and all, but I want to actually sleep. Not toss and turn, trying to find comfort all night."

"You slept just fine there last night." Of course he wants to make this an issue.

"Yes. When you were my pillow. Will you be joining me on the couch again?"

"No."

I nod triumphantly. "Then I will join you in this bed." He opens his mouth to respond, but I interrupt him. "You will have to physically move me. Which I know will be slight work for you, however, I will put up one hell of a fight if you try."

He raises a brow to my challenge. "Do you enjoy it?"

"What?" I side eye him.

"Being this annoying."

"You just told me earlier that you're happy you met me!"

"Doesn't mean you're not annoying."

"How is me sharing a bed with you annoying? Aren't we friends?"

"We are." He smiles. "You talk a lot though."

I sink into the bed with laughter. "All these truths you've been holding in. I was nervous and trying to smooth over the fact I pepper sprayed you."

"It made it worse." The smile he gives me lets me know he's full of shit.

"Whatever. We're here now. I tried to leave, and you insisted I stay. Enjoy me while you can. You can sleep alone when you get back to your place in Hope Valley."

"How long have you lived in Hope Valley?"

"My parents moved us there my senior year of high school. About ten years now. You?"

"Basically my whole life. We moved there in middle school. My mom lived there too until my dad passed. Then she wanted a fresh start. Now she's retired and travels from tropical place to tropical place."

"Ah," I sigh. "That sounds like the life."

"Why didn't you go somewhere warm for your getaway?"

"And miss a week with you? No, sir." He chuckles, settling into the pillows. "In all honesty, I was supposed to spend Christmas with my ex and his family in the Maldives. You know how that ended. Plus, I've been somewhere tropical every year for the past few years, and it never quite felt like Christmas."

"Yeah. You're right about that. Normally, that's where I go to avoid all this." He waves his hand, gesturing outside. "My assistant on the other hand, chose to be a pain in my ass."

I smile. "It's interesting how you pretend to be annoyed by everything, but you secretly enjoy it."

"How would you know that?" He turns on his side, propping himself up on his elbow.

"The reindeer today. I know you enjoyed it."

"When you're forced into something..."

"Forced? Please." I scoff. "Your reluctance is a front, Snow."

He watches me laugh with a smile on his face. "It was more fun than I thought it would be."

"Gotta get in touch with your inner child sometimes." Yawning, I reach toward the nightstand and turn off the lamp. Snow does the same. "Night, Snow."

"Night, Noelle." It's silent for a while. I think he's fallen asleep until his deep voice fills the room. "Given your name, do you like Christmas?"

"It's my favorite holiday. I was worried that it was going to be fucked up this year, but here I am stuck with a man who doesn't like it."

He chuckles. "You'll still enjoy yourself regardless of me."

"Damn right, I will. And drag you along with me in the process." I can't see his face in the dark, but I know he's smiling.

"Christmas was my dad's favorite holiday too. The decorations here are no match for how decked out our house would be."

I hear the warmth in his voice. "Do your siblings celebrate?"

"Yeah, my two brothers are visiting my mom. I used to go with them, but then I lost Kenna, and I just... couldn't."

I stare into the darkness. "You lost the love of your life. It's understandable."

"Yeah, but..." He lets out a sigh. "Never mind. I've talked about my dead fiancée enough."

I can't help my quiet laugh. "Say it."

"I wish I could enjoy myself like I used to. I'll be enjoying myself, for example our conversation now, and somehow my mind or the conversation will drift to her."

"I'm no therapist – "

"Shit, I'm sorry I didn't mean – "

I continue. "But you came on this trip, right? To this place that is the North Pole reincarnate." He laughs. "I can bet every last dollar that you're the type of person who won't do something they don't want to, no matter who it disappoints. You could be with your family, but you're here, stuck with me, a woman who loves Christmas and you're trying."

"True..." he says.

"Your mind and heart haven't caught up to the idea of moving on, but there's that flicker of desire for more. Until that turns into a flame, let things be what they are."

"You know..." I feel him shift beside me. "You're not half bad to talk to."

My brow furrows. "Um... we're going to have to work on your compliments."

He laughs heartily. "That was a statement. Not a compliment. A compliment would be me saying something like... you have the most captivating brown eyes."

My heart thrums in my chest. "Yeah," I say softly. "That's a compliment." His words make me feel seen. Something I haven't felt in a long time. "Thank you."

"Any time."

The next morning, I wake before Snow. Getting ready, I put on a long sleeve body suit, mom jeans, an oversized plaid shirt, and boots before pulling my hair into a bun. Grabbing my phone off the charger, I take it with me to start some coffee and check what events the resort has scheduled for today.

A little while later, Snow appears in the kitchen. He's wearing a long sleeve, black turtleneck that hugs his muscles, fitted jeans, and black combat style boots. I choke on my coffee. He wears black so fucking well even if I did talk shit about the lack of color in his wardrobe. Who looks this good first thing in the morning?

"You okay?" he asks as I succumb to a coughing fit due to the coffee I just choked down.

Catching my breath, I say, "Yeah, fine. You look good." My eyes widen as his brown eyes hold my gaze.

He gives me a panty melting smile. "So the black does it for you after all?"

"No," I shrug. "Still boring."

His laugh fills the kitchen. "Good thing I don't give a fuck about your opinion."

"You asked. I simply gave an answer."

"Where are you off to today? To cut wood?" His eyes are on my plaid shirt.

I give him my middle finger, finishing off my coffee. "I'm going to gingerbread making classes."

He leans against the counter, taking a bite of an apple. "Isn't that a couples class?"

"Yes." I stand at the sink, washing my cup. "But I figure there has to be some other single person there." Drying my hands, I turn to face him. "Hopefully said person is male and good looking."

He takes another bite of apple, chewing it slowly. "Yeah, you're probably right."

"What are your plans?"

He shrugs. "May hit the slopes. I don't know."

"You're always welcome to join me."

"What about the good looking guy you're hoping to be paired with?" He smirks, pushing away from the counter.

I shamelessly rake my eyes over him. "You'll do."

The smell of ginger, cinnamon, and clove permeate the air. Thankfully, Snow came with me. There wasn't a hot guy to help me make gingerbread. Instead, I'm watching Snow's arms flex as he rolls out the dough that was just pulled from the fridge. His sleeves are rolled up, exposing his forearms and the veins that are sexy for no reason.

"Did you want to try?"

I lick my lips, hoping I'm not drooling. "Sure."

He straightens up, holding the rolling pin out to me. When I grab it, he brings his hand to my cheek, rubbing his thumb along it. Goosebumps pepper my skin as I look up at him.

"You had some flour on your cheek."

"Oh…" I squeak, clearing my throat. "Thank you."

"You'll want to work quickly. The dough will get sticky otherwise and become hard to work with," the instructor announces to the class.

"You heard him." Snow leans against the counter. "Get to rolling. Can't have sticky cookies."

Narrowing my eyes, he gives me an amused look. Instead of arguing, I listen because I don't want to be the reason our cookies turn into a mess. The instructor brings around bins of cookie cutters while I finish rolling out the dough.

"What shapes do we want?" Snow asks from beside me, sorting through the cookie cutters.

"You choose." I set the rolling pin aside and peek in the box at the silver cookie cutters.

"It would be a crime to not have a gingerbread couple." He pulls out the gingerbread cutter, and I smile. "I also think we need reindeer to remember our reindeer date."

I blink at him, wondering if he meant to say that. It wasn't really a date. Was it? The pictures on my phone make it look like we're on a date. A date can be casual, right? I'm overthinking this. He has been flirting with me... I think. I haven't flirted with someone in a while. Maybe I'm reading him wrong.

"A Christmas tree, too," he says. "And do you want to do mittens or snowmen?"

"Snowmen." I smile, pulling myself out of my spiraling thoughts.

"Good choice." He pulls the cutter from the box.

We work side by side, cutting out gingerbread men, reindeer, Christmas trees, and snowmen. Once they're cut out and in the oven, the instructor passes out stuff to decorate the cookies.

"What would this couples class be without some friendly competition?" Laughter ripples through the room. Snow and I look at each other with smiles on our faces. "We'll be decorating our cookies. Whoever decorates the best cookie from the two of you, wins a ribbon and bragging rights. I will not be the only judge. Once you're done decorating, both of you will choose the cookie you'd like to be judged. Then me and your classmates will vote for the best cookie out of each couple. Remember," He holds up his hands. "This is friendly. I don't want to hear of anyone being put out in the snow tonight."

"That blue ribbon is mine." I give Snow a smug smile.

"Such confidence." He pats my shoulder.

I brush his hand off me. "Care to make a friendly wager?"

"Are you sure you want to do this?"

"It's a yes or no question, Snow."

He smiles, crossing his arms and leans against the counter. "Yes. What are you going to do for me, Noelle?"

"Wow, you're arrogant too?" The corners of his mouth tip up. "That's a trait that could've stayed hidden."

"Tell me what you're going to do for me."

Anything with him talking to me like that.

"You," I poke at his chest, "will be streaking through that snow that's falling outside."

"Streaking?" He looks out the window. "In this weather? Are you sure?"

"Scared?" I ask.

"For you? Yes. But if that's what you want to wager, I'll enjoy watching you run naked through the snow with a hot mug of cocoa in my hands."

"We'll see," I say smugly.

Once the cookies have cooled, we begin decorating. Snow nudges me out of the way when I try to reach for the decorations. I elbow his side, making him laugh and move out of my way. Honestly, I don't know what I was thinking with this bet. What if he can decorate a cookie? I'll be ass out. Literally.

I'm not off to a good start when I struggle to put the frosting into the piping bag. Snow does this effortlessly while smiling at me. I don't let on that I'm bothered by this show. Instead, I take my tray of cookies over to the other counter and turn my back to him. The first few cookies are terrible. My lines are shaky and in some areas I squeezed out too much frosting. I save the reindeer and gingerbread man for last.

"Five minutes," the instructor announces.

"What?" I gasp, looking up at the clock.

It's been almost an hour since we started decorating. Snow chuckles behind me. I'm tempted to go look at his cookies, but I need to focus on making the last two fucking amazing. The gingerbread man doesn't turn out bad or good. I'm happy with the reindeer though. It looks Pinterest worthy.

"Time's up. Please choose which cookie you'd like to be judged and bring it up with your partner."

I plate my reindeer cookie and finally take a peek at Snow's cookies. Letting out a gasp, I nearly drop my plate.

"You fucking bamboozled me!" He laughs indulgently. "Who are you? Martha Stewart's protégé?" I stare at his intricately decorated plate of cookies.

"You never asked if I've baked. My mom and dad were basically Mr. and Mrs. Claus. Baking was a tradition in our house for the holidays."

Despite being cheated, my heart warms as he shares this memory with me. "I cannot believe you."

"Hey." He holds his hands up in front of him. "I asked if you were sure about this."

I brush away his statement with a wave of my hand. "I thought you were being arrogant."

"Nah. That's all you, sweetheart." He turns his head to the side, looking at my cookie. "It looks good."

I narrow my eyes at him. "You tell such pretty lies." His reindeer has detailed eyes, nose, and antlers with fucking lights on them.

"Seriously, Noelle. It looks good."

"Yeah, yeah." I march to the front, putting my sketchy reindeer up to be judged. Snow places his beside mine. Looking up at him, I shake my head, and he shrugs innocently.

It's easy to see that Snow's cookie is the best of them all. I'm still going to hold out hope that somehow my cookie wins. The snow is still falling outside with no signs of stopping anytime soon.

"Take these pieces of paper," the instructor says, holding up strips of paper. "Write down cookie one or two and drop it in the box in front of the cookies to cast your vote."

There are twelve couples in total. It doesn't take long for us to cast our votes. While we wait for the instructor to tally them up, we eat gingerbread cookies and talk with the other couples.

"Is this your first time here?" The man of the couple who was baking beside us asks.

"Yeah," Snow and I say in unison.

"You two are in sync," the woman says with a chuckle. "How long have you been together?"

"We're friends," I say.

"You two could've fooled me." She smiles brightly.

I look at Snow. He doesn't seem bothered this time by someone mistaking us for a couple. He smiles at me before taking a bite of his cookie.

"Alright, I've placed blue ribbons by the winning cookies. Thank you for creating memories with me today. Enjoy your stays and happy holidays!" He smiles.

I internally groan, knowing I should've kept my mouth shut about the "friendly wager".

"Ready to strip for me?" Snow asks.

His words make me aware of the pulse between my thighs. I mean... things could be worse. Running through the snow with his eyes on me won't be too bad. Offering my body up as sacrifice to him seems like a small price to pay.

"We haven't even looked yet."

I don't need to see the blue ribbon beside his cookie to know he won. I am happy to see that I did get some votes though. My cookie wasn't as bad as I thought and that makes me smile.

"Hey, I got some votes."

"I told you it wasn't bad." He smiles. "Now," he tucks a loose braid behind my ear, "are you ready to strip for me?"

This is *definitely* flirting. "I hate that I am a woman of my very stupid word." He laughs. "But can we eat first? A gingerbread cookie isn't gonna do it for me."

"Yeah, you'll need your energy for later." He winks at me before walking out of the class and I follow behind him.

9
Noelle

ARRIVING AT THE CABIN, I shrug out of my coat. We stayed longer than expected after eating, walking through the little village that makes up Mistletoe Mountain resort. It felt like we were in a Christmas movie. This place is magical. I open a bottle of wine, pouring myself a glass. Snow sits in front of the fire, scrolling through his phone. Grabbing my glass, I head to the bedroom with the intent of fulfilling the bet I made. It's still snowing outside. Could I back out of this? Yes, but where's the fun in that? I came here to have fun, and I'm going to have it.

Digging through my suitcase, I look for my leather gloves and fur hat. I'll wear my Moon Boots for good measure. Stripping out of my clothes, I head into the bathroom for a robe and tie it around myself. It's fluffy, cozy, and warm. I put on some thick wool socks and then pull on my Moon Boots. Taking my braids out of their bun, I put on my hat and slip on the leather gloves. If I'm being honest, I look cute. Finishing my glass of wine, I head out to the living room.

"Prepare yourself," I say dramatically.

"For what?" he asks without looking up from his phone.

"For me to run naked in the snow." I stand in front of him.

He looks up at me. "Nice hat."

"Thank you." I smile, putting my foot up on the ottoman. My robe falls open, exposing my leg.

His eyes trail down my leg, tossing his head back with laughter when he sees my Moon Boots. "Seriously?"

"Yes." I laugh with him. "You hate on these, but they're warm and cute. Fuck what you say."

"I don't know. You could change my mind tonight." His eyes meet mine, and my cheeks warm. I'll be sweating by the time I get outside if he keeps talking to me like that. "Let me make myself a cup of cocoa first. I want to fully enjoy this experience."

"Take your time. I'm not trying to freeze my tits off any faster than I have to." He laughs his way to the kitchen.

Fifteen minutes later, Snow has his cocoa, and I'm leading the way outside. It's still snowing, just not as heavily. Turning to him, I hand him my phone.

"Take pictures of me."

"Naked?" His full lips part as he stares at me.

"Yeah, Snow. Naked."

"If that's what you want…" Pulling off his glove with his teeth, he grabs my phone. I take the glove from his mouth and put it in his jacket pocket. "Thanks," he says.

While he's opening the camera, I take off my robe.

"Okay. I'm re – damn." His eyes are on my ass. That reaction makes this worth it. I toss the robe over his shoulder.

"Don't forget the pictures, or I'll kick you in the balls if I have to do this again."

"Right." He blinks, struggling to look at my eyes as they flit between me and my breasts. "Ready when you are."

My teeth are already chattering. I take off running. This is probably–no, it *is* –the dumbest, most exhilarating thing I've done. I stop about ten feet away from Snow, holding my arms out to the side, and spin on the spot. Standing with my tongue out, I let the snowflakes melt on it. If I could suspend myself in this moment, and not die from hypothermia, I would. The world is so quiet it feels like it's just me and Snow in it. I smile back at him. This getaway has turned into so much more than I thought it would be. I feel like I've done more with Snow in the past two and a half days than I ever did with Malcolm in three years. I doubt anything romantic will develop with Snow, but hopefully, after all of this, we can be friends at least.

Now that I'm thoroughly frozen, I make my way back to him. He's too busy staring at my tits, taking pictures, to notice I have a snowball in my hand. Rolling it in my palms to make it firm, I launch it at his face. His eyes widen when it hits him. I run like hell for the cabin, laughing hysterically.

"Noelle!" he growls.

As I'm running up the steps, a snowball hits my ass. I double over with laughter, trying to breathe. He wraps his arm around my waist, pulling me back.

"You didn't plan this well did you, Snowflake?" He flips me over his shoulder as if I weigh nothing.

I'm laughing too hard to respond. He walks us toward a blanket of snow. "How well can you make a snow angel?"

"N-no, n-no!" Being hit with a snowball is one thing, but dumping me in a snow drift is cruel and unusual punishment. "I'm going to d-die from hy-hypothermia." My lungs burn from taking gasps of ice cold air.

"Apologize," he says, standing in front of the snowbank.

"N-no." I say, calling his bluff. If he was going to toss me in, he would've done it by now.

He shocks me when he grabs a handful of snow, smacking my ass. I gasp, biting my lip, and grab fistfuls of his jacket. Why the fuck did that feel so unnecessarily good? I squeeze my thighs together.

"Apologize."

"I-I c-can't ap-poligze f-for s-something I-I'm n-n-not s-sorry f-for," I stutter.

"Still with that bullshit?"

He pulls me over his shoulder, carrying me bridal style, getting ready to drop me in the snowbank.

"W-w-wait! P-put m-me d-down f-f-first."

"Uh uh. I wanna hear the words, Snowflake. Or I drop you in this snowbank."

I wrap my arms so tight around his neck that we'll go down together if he tries anything. "I-I'm s-sorry for-r h-having s-such g-good aim-m-m," I stutter through chattering teeth.

Amusement lights his eyes as I look up at him. "Willing to talk shit even when on the brink of hypothermia?"

"Y-y-yessss." I can't really tell if I'm smiling because my lips are numb. "P-please t-take m-meee ins-side."

He stands in front of the snowbank for a few seconds longer before turning around and heading for the cabin. I've never been this cold in my life. Once we're inside, he sets me down near the fire. My body doesn't feel like my own it's so unbelievably numb. He grabs a blanket off the back of the couch, wrapping it around my shoulders. Taking off his jacket, he pulls his shirt over his head. He wraps his arms around me, pulling me against his warm chest. I hold onto his middle. I'd wrap my whole body around him if I could. He feels so good. We stand by the fire, my cheek pressed against his chest, until my shivering calms down.

"I hope you know that was a really stupid idea." His voice resonates in his chest.

I laugh softly. "I k-know, but it was f-fun, no?"

He's silent for a few breaths. "It was." There's a smile in his tone.

"Did you g-get pictures?" A shiver runs through me.

"Damn... I forgot."

"Snow!" I try to pull away, but he wraps his arms tightly around me.

"I'm kidding. I got pictures of you running ass out in the snow until you threw that snowball in my face." I snort with laughter. "You're lucky I'm a gentleman."

"Thank you for letting me do stupid shit and then making sure I don't die."

"Any time. To be completely honest, I was looking forward to this part. If your dumb shit leads to situations like this, I will gladly be a bystander."

I lift my head meeting his gaze. His eyes drop to my lips. I can finally feel them again, and they're tingling to kiss him. Pressing up onto my tiptoes, he leans forward, when we're an inch from each other, his phone slices through the moment. He rests his forehead against mine.

"That's my brother. I've gotta take it or he'll keep calling."

I sink back down to my feet, pulling away from him, and wrap the blanket around me tightly. "Yeah, of course."

He clears his throat, answering his phone. While he talks, I head to the room for my bikini. The hot tub is calling my name. I toss my hat and gloves onto the bed, slipping off my boots while I dig in my suitcase. Snow has already seen everything – twice – a bikini seems silly. But I don't know if he'll join me or not. I know how it is having siblings, Aspen will blow up my phone if I miss a call. She's let me have my peace on this vacation, only checking in through text messages and by sending me pictures of her with Eve. They'd be proud of me tonight.

Tying the strings of my bikini, I reenter the living room . Snow is in deep conversation with his brother, until he sees me.

"North, let me call you later." His eyes trail up my body. "That's great," he says to his brother. "Bye." He tosses his phone aside. "Where are you going?"

"Thought I'd make snow angels before bed." His brown eyes meet mine, and he has a smirk on his lips. "Kidding. You couldn't pay me to go back out there. I'm getting in the hot tub."

"No invitation?" he asks, rising to his feet.

"You're a grown ass man, Snow. Invite yourself." I shrug my shoulder, continuing on my way.

I hope he invites himself. He's been flirting with me all day, and we nearly kissed. His brother would choose that moment to call. If that were Aspen, I'd punch her in the boob when I got home.

I press the button on the hot tub's control panel, turning it on. The hot tub is in a small room with glass walls and an incredible view. I'm convinced this place is stunning from every angle. I turn off the lights, appreciating the night sky. I submerge myself up to my neck in the warm, bubbling water, letting out a sigh. For the first time in a long time, I can confidently say I'm happy. These past couple of days with Snow have been wonderful. He steps into the tub at the same time he enters my thoughts, sitting beside me. The stars had to align just right for him to be my cabin mate.

"Careful, or you'll melt, Snowflake."

"Is that my new name?" I ask with a smile.

"May as well be. My name is Snow and I've never run naked in it."

"It kinda feels like you have to do it now."

"Not gonna happen." He smiles. "I'm here for the views and pictures."

"How's your brother?"

"Good. Just wanted to see how I was doing. Your sister hasn't called you?"

"Hell no. And I'm thankful she hasn't "

He chuckles. "Why?"

I shift my body toward him. "She and my best friend thought I'd go off the deep end after the breakup. They think I'm hiding my feelings. I cried about it, but I really just feel... free. It's hard to explain."

"I get it." He nods his head.

"You do?" I tilt my head to the side, raising a brow.

"Yeah. I had one other serious relationship before Kenna. We dated for two years. When it was over, I was sad, but relieved. She and I were more friends than lovers. It worked out best for both of us. She got married shortly after our split."

"Did that bother you? That she got married so soon."

"Nah." He shrugs. "I wish her nothing but the best. She got married, and I met Kenna. Even if I hadn't met Kenna, I still wouldn't harbor any resentment."

I watch the bubbles whirl around in the water. "I hated Malcolm initially, but he did us both a favor. Do I wish it would've happened differently? Yeah, but life has an interesting way of working itself out."

"It does," he agrees. "We probably wouldn't have met otherwise."

Looking at him, I smile. He feels closer than he was seconds ago. Moving forward, he closes the gap between us. I notice the paintbrush of freckles across the bridge of his nose. His lashes are thick and jet black, like his hair. Why is it that boys get the best lashes and brows? They could care less and –

Snow's lips meet mine. The kiss is soft, gentle... slow. The aimless, reeling thoughts are silenced and replaced with blazing desire. Just as I'm leaning into the kiss he pulls away. My eyes flutter open.

"Sorry..." He smooths his hand over his beard.

"For... what?"

"Kissing you. I know you just got out of a relationship and – "

"The only thing on my mind is this..." I cup his face in my hands, bringing his lips to mine again.

It's the confirmation he needs, slipping his hand around the back of my neck, pulling me flush against him. I moan into his mouth. Kissing him is better than I imagined. His lips are plush and soft. Teasing my lips with his tongue, I open for him, letting our tongues dance. Snow tastes like... mint. He brushed his teeth before joining me? Which means he... intended to kiss me? It makes butterflies flicker to life in my stomach, realizing I'm not delusional. He *was* flirting with me and wanted this too.

He trails kisses along my jaw, nipping just below my earlobe. His strong hands glide over my body, pulling me onto his lap. Straddling him, I press my center against the growing stiffness in his swim trunks, giving me a jolt of pleasure. He slips his hands into my bikini bottoms, gripping my ass, and I roll my hips to feel the pressure on my center again. Snow groans, making goosebumps pepper my skin.

Turning us around, he grips my waist, hoisting me up onto the hot tub's ledge. I press my palms into the floor, leaning back, keeping my feet and calves in the water.

I give him a bemused expression. He lit me up. I hope he isn't dousing the flames. His eyes lock onto mine as a sexy smirk appears on his lips.

Plucking up one of the strings on my bikini bottoms, he asks, "Can I have a taste?"

I nearly combust. He can have it all. A taste, meal, and a fucking feast complete with dessert.

I part my legs, and he stands between my thighs. "Be my guest." My heart races.

I watch him with bated breath as he pulls on the string still in his hold, untying it. He grips my hip, caressing it, as his thumb massages the crease between my thigh and center. Undoing the other side, he tugs, exposing me. Snow inhales sharply. Biting my bottom lip, I smile. Holding my gaze, he sinks into the hot tub until he's level with my pussy. Pulling me to the edge, he grips my thighs spreading them apart and pushes my legs up so my toes dangle in the water.

"Keep them up and open for me." He doesn't have to tell me twice. "And for the record," He dips his fingers into my wetness, licking them clean. "I like my cookies sticky."

My lips part as I gape at him. Has he been thinking about this moment since our gingerbread class? He steals my breath when his tongue meets my center. My toes curl, my back arches, and I let out a needy moan. He does this without being asked? I can count on one hand the number of times Malcolm went down on me.

Snow is happily licking his way to my fucking soul.

His hand glides up my body, pulling at the strings around my neck, exposing my breasts. I gasp when he twirls my nipple between his fingertips.

"Fuck, Snow. You feel so good." I bask in the pleasure.

Just when I think he can't take me any higher, he slides his fingers deep into my wetness, massaging an area that makes my body quake. I let out a shuddering moan that echoes off the walls. Placing my hand on his head, I grab a fistful of his curls. Our eyes lock when I look down at him between my thighs. He's my undoing.

Pleasure courses through my body. Tipping my head back, I look out the window and swear I see a shooting star. Or maybe I'm just seeing stars. Snow wraps his hand around my throat, bringing my gaze back to his. Keeping his tongue on my clit, I'm surprised when I feel another orgasm building in my core.

"Again?" I whimper. "Again. I'm coming again."

His deep chuckle vibrates in my center. The orgasm hits me like a wave, pulling me under. My hips buck, and Snow grips my waist to keep me from falling while I fall apart for him. The shockwaves that follow have impassioned moans spilling from my lips. He swirls his tongue around my clit as the last waves ripple through me.

Rising to his feet, he pulls me off the edge, and I wrap my arms around his neck and legs around his waist. He grips my thighs, carrying us both out of the water.

"Where are you taking me?" I rest my head in the crook of his neck.

"To shower. Then to bed. Unless you're ready for bed?"

"A shower with you sounds nice," I mutter. There's something about a man carrying a woman as if she weighs nothing that will always do it for me. I wrap myself around him tighter.

Reaching the bathroom, he sets me down, grabbing the shower cap off the counter, and covers my hair *and* eyes.

I snort with laughter, adjusting the cap. "Almost thought you were sweet for a moment."

"Can't have you thinking that." He smiles, turning on the water. When he faces me, there's a look of concern in his eyes. "Um... I don't want to ruin the moment but I wasn't anticipating you being here. I don't have any condoms and – "

"Hold that thought." I say, running out of the bathroom, tearing through my bag. When my hand lands on the box of condoms, I dart back into the bathroom. "I'm on birth control and have condoms." I think I'll kiss Eve when I get back.

Tilting his head to the side, there's a hint of a smirk on his lips. "I can see that."

I open the box, taking one out. "My best friend really thinks I need to–"

He crashes into me, kissing me with such intensity I'm not sure where I end and he begins. Pulling away, he says, "I'm going to have to personally thank her."

Steam fills the bathroom. Grabbing the waistband of his shorts, he pulls them down. My eyes take all of him in. I've seen my fair share of dicks, but his is the first to make me wet from the sight and my mouth water. If his tongue catapulted me into ecstasy, I can only imagine what he'll do with the length and girth hanging between his legs. Hopefully I don't have to imagine for long.

Taking my hand, he leads me into the steamy shower. We stand under the warm waterfall for a moment, sliding his hand around the back of my neck, he brings his lips to mine. I get lost in the kiss, taking the opportunity to feel on his chest and abs. Backing us up, he presses me against the wall, trailing kisses down my neck, nipping at my collar bone. His hand glides down my body until his fingertips find my center, massaging. I hum with pleasure, spreading my legs for him. When my hand wraps around his length, he grunts, resting his forehead against mine as I stroke him.

Pressing a kiss to his lips, I say, "I need you inside me."

"You're ready?" He gently nips my bottom lip.

"Yes," I breathe out.

Sitting on the bench that's built into the wall, I watch him roll on the condom before he pulls me toward him. The way his eyes drink me in as if I was made for him makes my body tingle with wanton desire. Gliding his hand over my stomach, he cups my breast, squeezing it. I rest my hand on his shoulder as I straddle his lap. He takes my nipple into his mouth, sucking on it, and gently grazing his teeth against it before doing the same to the other. I moan, letting my head fall back as he kisses my chest and neck. His dick presses against my center and I ache to feel him inside me.

Reaching down between us, I wrap my hand around him. He takes a sharp inhale of breath, gripping my hips, as I stroke him and glide the tip of his dick along my wetness. His brown eyes hold my gaze as I slowly lower myself onto him. When he's nearly buried inside me, I close my eyes.

He slides his hand up my throat, applying light pressure. "Look at me." I listen, looking at him with hazy eyes. "I want to watch you take all of me." In one swift thrust, he buries himself. My breath hitches as his eyes burn with desire. "That's a good girl, breathe deep, take all of it."

"You're gonna be the end of me." I let out a strangled cry of pleasure as he stretches me out.

With his hand still wrapped around my throat, he pulls me toward him. "Not quite." He whispers in my ear. "We've only just begun."

He moves his hips, gripping my waist, making me bounce on him. Putting my hands on his shoulders, I match his thrusts, feeling the steady build of a climax. I lean back slightly and he hits the spot that makes my toes curl. Bringing his hand between us, he presses his thumb against my clit. Seconds later, I'm biting down on his shoulder, coming undone for him again.

"Snow..." I moan as my body trembles.

"Cum on this dick, Noelle..." he grits out.

Snow is so reserved, I wouldn't have imagined he'd have his hand around my throat, talking to me in this way.

"Harder, deeper..." I cry out. My eyes roll back in my head as I shut them, caught in his rapture.

He delivers, thrusting so deep into me that I see stars and bursts of color. The moans spill from my lips, and he swallows them as he kisses me. Wrapping his arms around my waist, keeping me flush against him, he thrusts harder. I hold onto him, teetering on the edge of another orgasm.

"Fuck, I can't stop coming..." I moan.

"Give it to me, Noelle. Every last fucking drop..." He enunciates each word with the thrust of his hips. He plunges into me, opening the flood gates, as if he's had the key this whole time.

I let out a guttural moan, falling into bliss. He continues to thrust into me, chasing his own release.

His body trembles. I lean back, resting my hands on his thighs as I match his thrusts. He holds onto my waist.

"Noelle, I'm going to – "

"Cum for me."

He pulls me flush against him, letting out a mix of a moan and a growl as he spills into me. I feel his dick twitch with his release, and I move my hips to get all of it. He rests his head on my chest as we come down from our high. I press a kiss to his wet curls. After a few moments of catching our breath, he reaches for the soap, lathering it onto me.

I stare at him as he watches his hands glide over my body. How has a man I met days ago shown me more care and attention than a person I spent three years with?

"You okay?" he asks, rising to his feet, putting us both upright.

"Yeah." I stand, feeling like my body is made of jello. "I just... you're a generous lover, you know that, right?"

A chuckle rumbles in his chest. "Isn't that the whole point of sex? To give and receive pleasure?"

"Yeah, but... you're telling me sex is *always* like that for you?"

He closes his eyes as the stream of water drenches his curls, running over his face. "Honestly," he says as he opens his eyes with water clinging to his lashes. They're swirling with emotion. "Not always. Just with you."

10
SNOW

AFTER GOING A FEW more rounds in bed, Noelle fell asleep. Now I'm holding her in my arms as I see the first rays of light peeking out from behind the mountain. I'd be lying if I said I hadn't imagined burying myself inside her from the moment I saw her brown eyes. I thought it was going to be like every other hookup I'd experienced in the past five years – meaningless. Instead, I felt like she ignited a dormant flame inside of me. I've spent the past few hours lost in my head, realizing I've never felt this connected to someone. Then the thought filled me with guilt. Kenna meant everything to me, but this with Noelle is different. I don't know how it's possible after meeting her only days ago.

Noelle startles me when she sits up abruptly with one eye open. "What's your last name?"

"What?" My brows pinch together.

"Your last name. What is it?"

"You woke up out of your sleep to ask me that question?" I try to keep the smile off my face.

"Yes." She nods matter-of-factly, closing her eyes.

"King." I watch as she licks her lips, trying to hide a smile.

"Seriously?" She focuses on me. "King? Snow King?" Falling onto my chest, she cackles.

"I knew your punk ass was going to laugh." Wrapping my arms around her, I press a kiss to her temple.

"Snow King. It's too perfect. With your ego, I'm surprised you don't throw that around more often."

"I don't have an ego."

"You told me you don't make mistakes. Mr. King, if that's not ego, what is it?"

"The truth. Is this cabin not rightfully mine?"

"Truth or not. It's called ego."

"Do you always wake up swinging? Or is that just this morning?"

"No, just this morning. It's also hard for me to fall back asleep once awake."

"I have a remedy for that."

She rests her chin on my chest, looking up at me. "And that remedy is?"

Sitting up, I flip her onto her back. The look of appetency in her eyes makes my dick twitch. I watch her chest heave with anticipation.

I chuckle, positioning myself between her thighs. "I haven't even touched you yet..."

"You only ever had to touch me once for me to know."

I press kisses along her inner thighs, watching as she gets wetter with each one. Sliding my hands underneath her ass, pulling her toward me, I push her thighs further apart with my shoulders.

She covers her eyes with her arm, smiling. "You're teasing me and that's – "

I don't understand the next word. It gets lost in her throat as I devour her center.

I'm watching Noelle bend over naked while she digs through her suitcase. Maybe I am a voyeur after all. I could watch her all day. Licking multiple orgasms out of her led to me being buried inside her again, and then we slept the morning away.

"What does your friend like? We should send her something so I can properly express my gratitude."

She smiles, putting on her bra. "She won't accept it, but she'll be thrilled to know I am thoroughly enjoying my vacation."

"I was prepared to risk it all if you gave me the green light."

"Damn." She falls into a fit of laughter as she pulls up her panties. "I can tell that was heavy on your mind."

I grin, laughing with her. "For the record, I always use condoms. I'm not reckless... but with the way *you* look and taste. I wanted to be all on your curves. Fuck the brakes."

"If it means anything, consequences of recklessness weren't a thought in my mind. I'd risk it all too."

I'm not sure a child with her would be a consequence. Okay, I've *really* lost my shit. "Do you want kids?" The question is out of my mouth before I can stop myself.

"I do." She smiles. "Six of them."

My jaw goes slack. "Six?"

Her laughter fills the room. "You should see your face. Nah, like two or three. I know my limits. You?"

"Yeah. I do. Two or three sounds good."

I stare into her brown eyes as she holds my gaze. There's a glimmer of something in them. It makes me wonder if she's feeling the same way I am or if this really is just a vacation hookup. Before I can give it too much thought, she clears her throat, pulling away, and grabs some jeans.

"What are you doing today?"

"Whatever you're doing."

"Aw!" She smiles coyly. "You like spending time with me?"

I don't want to assume that we'll see each other when we get back to Hope Valley, so I'll enjoy the time we have together now. "You're alright."

She giggles, playfully pushing my arm. "I want to go on a sleigh ride, but it was full when I made my reservation, so I was going to bother Nicholas to see if he'll make something happen for me."

"I'll pray for him."

"Fuck you. He likes me." She puts on a sweater with a zipper in the front that hugs her breasts just right. "I should have you talk to him. He about shit himself when you were on your cabin crusade the other day."

"He shouldn't have fucked up." I tear my eyes away from her cleavage. "But if you want to go on a sleigh ride, I'll get you a sleigh ride whether Nicholas helps or not."

"Let's go then, Mr. King." She interlaces her fingers with mine. I can't help but to feel like our hands were made to fit together.

In the lobby, Noelle leans against the counter, talking to Nicholas. He's about our age or maybe a couple of years older. I think he likes Noelle for more reasons than she cares to realize. Or maybe she realizes it and is currently using it to her advantage to get what she wants.

He glances at her cleavage before looking at me, and then becomes more interested in getting Noelle her sleigh ride. "Of course, Miss Frost. Anything for you." He types away on his keyboard. "Can you believe it's Christmas Eve tomorrow?"

Noelle looks surprised by this news. "It is?" She glances at me over her shoulder. "Lost track of time. I've been enjoying my stay."

"You two have been getting along well then?" Nicholas looks between the two of us.

She straightens up, pressing her palms into the counter, and shrugs her shoulders. "We're getting acquainted. Snow is very... accommodating."

I let out a low, smooth chuckle. "It's my pleasure."

Noelle crosses her legs, squeezing her thighs together. No doubt remembering me being between them all last night and this morning.

"Happy to hear." Nicholas smiles. "There was a cancellation this morning. The sleigh will pick you up in an hour at your cabin. It will then take you on a ride up the mountain ending with a campfire complete with s'mores and a gorgeous view of Mistletoe Mountain."

Noelle bounces with excitement. "Thank you so much, Nicholas. I'll leave you alone now." She steps to the side, letting the people behind us check in.

"You're not a bother. Enjoy your day."

Turning around, she smiles at me, looping her arm through mine. "Ready for this sleigh ride?"

Her excitement is infectious, making it hard to not enjoy my time here. "I am."

A cardinal red sleigh pulls up an hour later, pulled by a majestic chestnut colored horse with a flaxen colored mane and tail. Noelle's eyes are alight with excitement. She's helping me rediscover the wonder and magic of Christmas again. Even if we don't see each other after this trip, I'll take what she's given back to me and cherish it for the rest of my days. Holding out my hand, I help her climb onto the sleigh and then follow behind her.

"Welcome." The driver smiles. "We'll go a mile and half up the mountain. It typically takes between thirty to forty minutes. Enjoy the ride."

"Thank you." I smile.

Resting my arm on the back of the bench, Noelle snuggles closer to me. "Your body is much warmer than mine." She smiles.

"I'm not going to complain."

The sleigh takes off. Noelle tosses her head back with laughter, sticking her tongue to catch the falling snowflakes.

"Try it." She nudges my arm, sticking her tongue out again.

I side eye her. "The only snowflake I want on my tongue is you."

She blinks with her tongue still hanging out of her mouth. I chuckle, watching a snowflake land on her tongue. Leaning forward, I snake my hand around the back of her neck, and press my tongue to hers, tasting the snowflake. Her eyes close, kissing me back. For a few breaths, I get lost in the feel and taste of her.

Pulling away, she has a dazed look on her face. "I caught one..." I mutter.

Eventually she comes back to the present. A slow smile spreads across her lips as she looks at the scenery passing us by. The trees and the snow fall have become denser. Wilder was right – this place is stunning.

"I know you don't celebrate Christmas, but do you do anything special?" Noelle asks.

"Just a trip. I'd rather be alone with my thoughts than my family waiting for me to have an emotional breakdown."

"Do you... have an emotional breakdown?" she asks with sincerity in her voice.

"I was a mess the first few years. I mean I guess I still am a mess some days – " she laughs softly " – but things hurt a little less with time. The emotions are still strong, but they're not as debilitating as they were. But now? Nah. I just like to be alone."

"I can give you space if you need it. I'm sure you're tired of me dragging you around to all this festive stuff."

"Can't really drag a willing participant, can you?"

She looks at me with a sly smile. "So you have enjoyed yourself?"

"I've enjoyed you." All the stuff she's "dragged" me to, I've enjoyed because of *her*. She looks down at her hands with a smile still on her face. "What about you? Any traditions?"

"Basic stuff. Christmas Eve is more festive. Dinner, drinking, games, movies, and whatever else. Christmas Day is a lot more chill with opening presents and a big dinner."

"Sounds like my family." I smile.

"Does your mom still go all out for Christmas decorations?"

"Carol King would *never* allow someone to upstage her on Christmas." Noelle grins. "She does it in honor of my dad now. Not just for the glory of having the best decorated house."

"I would love to see that! That's one of the best things about Christmas. All the decked out houses."

I'm not sure if she means she'd really love to see my mom's house or if she's just being nice. "When she's not traveling, she lives in Sapphire Shores. Have you been?" Sapphire Shores is a costal town and is a twelve hour drive from Hope Valley. Two if you fly.

"I have, but it was years ago on a family trip. Do you visit her often?"

"I do. Every couple of months, and in between she'll come spend time with my brothers and me."

"You're close then?"

Nodding, I smile. "Very close knit. What about you and your family?"

"Yeah, my family is like that too. My sister is my best friend. We lived together at one point."

My brow furrows. "What happened?"

"Met my ex, we got an apartment together a year after dating."

I still don't understand how he cheated on her even if they were on the fritz. After a few days in her presence, I couldn't imagine intentionally going out of my way to hurt Noelle. He must be a real piece of shit.

"Where do you work?" she asks.

"Have you heard of North Star Toys?"

"Yes!" Her face lights up, and I chuckle. "Basically I'm a big ass kid, if you couldn't tell, and I'm never growing up like Peter Pan. I love going there. They have the best Christmas displays. What do you do there?"

"My family owns it..."

She gasps, gripping my arm as she stares at me with wide eyes. "Are you serious?"

"I am. My dad started the company and then my brothers and I took over it after he passed."

Her eyes grow even larger, making me laugh, and she pats my arm rapidly. "Kingmaker Toys. That's your brand?"

"My family's brand, yes."

"This is... wild. I wasn't expecting you to own a whole toy company. Do you and your brothers manage it together?"

"Yes. We all have different roles though."

"What's yours?"

"CEO. I took over when my dad passed."

"CEO?" Her eyes widen and I love watching the delight dance in her eyes. "Really? You're so..."

"So?" I raise a brow, cocking my head to the side.

"Serious. I'd imagine the CEO of a toy company to be goofy and child-like."

I chuckle. "I'm just quiet. That's how my dad was though. There was never a dull moment in my childhood."

"Can I ask what– "

"Happened to him?" I finish for her.

"Yeah..." She grabs my hand. "You don't have to talk about it if you don't want to."

"I don't mind talking about him with you. My dad, Chris, died from a brain aneurysm ten years ago." She squeezes my hand, and I see tears in her eyes. Noelle is the first person I've met who cries for someone she barely knows.

"After he passed, our mom told us he'd been having health issues that my parents kept from us. They were things that could be fixed with lifestyle changes. He was retiring and had plans to take better care of himself. I was twenty-three and still in college, but dropped everything to go home and support my family."

She gives me a sympathetic smile. "Did you want to run the company?"

"Ugh..." I look at the pine trees, zipping by. "That's a really loaded question."

"Oh," She cringes. "Sorry."

"Nah. It's okay. It's just... I'm the middle child. My brother Winter is the oldest and was supposed to take over when our dad retired. Then he passed unexpectedly and Winter was... lost. He still kind of is. I took over because I didn't want us to lose our dad's company after losing him. I knew I'd do something at North Star Toys, but I didn't imagine I would be the CEO. Because it was Winter's dream, you know?"

I thought I'd be doing something like North, working behind the scenes in finance or marketing like Winter is now. It's grown on me even if it wasn't what I imagined for myself. I was apprehensive when I took on the role, but I always feel a sense of pride knowing I'm taking care of what my dad built for our family.

"That's a big responsibility to take on."

"It was, but I enjoy it now. It's a fun job when it's not stressing me out."

"You're happy then?" The corners of her mouth tip up.

In this moment, looking into her brown eyes, "Yeah, I am."

The sleigh slows down as we come to a small clearing with a fire and a picnic setup. When Noelle sees it, she squeals, making me toss my head back with laughter.

"Isn't it so cute?"

When the sleigh comes to a stop, I get off and then help Noelle, putting my hands around her waist and setting her on the snow covered ground.

"I'll be in the stable," The driver points to a small building not too far from the fire. "We'll be here for about an hour while the horse rests and you two enjoy the refreshments."

"Thank you." Noelle smiles brightly.

"You're also welcome to come get me before the hour if you're ready to go back sooner. I'll let you two enjoy your time." The driver takes off again.

"Isn't this utter perfection?" Noelle spins on the spot before walking toward the fire.

"It's nice."

A log has been carved out to look like a bench with a Pendleton blanket slung over it. Sitting atop a small sled off to the side is a bucket with chocolate bars, marshmallows, graham crackers, stuff for hot cocoa, and a bottle of rum.

Noelle wastes no time, sitting in front of the fire, and putting a marshmallow onto a skewer to roast it. Sitting beside her, I grab the silver pot, pouring the milk and cream into it before placing it over the fire.

"You've made cocoa over a fire before?"

Chuckling, I nod my head. "Yes."

"Should've known." She smiles, pulling her flaming marshmallow from the fire, and blows it out. "Did you want one?"

"Yeah. I'll take one, please."

"How would you like your marshmallow? Warm, slightly toasted, or burned?" Taking off the crispy outer layer of the marshmallow, she puts it into her mouth, closing her eyes as she chews.

"Burned." Pulling the milk and cream from the fire before it starts to boil, I grab the chocolate and put the crumbled pieces into the pot to melt.

"Seriously?" She scrunches up her face.

"Yes, seriously." I laugh. "I like my marshmallows burned on the outside and gooey on the inside."

"Alright," she sighs. "One burned, gooey s'more coming up."

"I like what I like. You already know I like things better when they're sticky." Stirring the hot cocoa, I feel her eyes on me. Turning to meet her gaze, she's forgotten about my marshmallow as she stares at me. "I said burned. Not charred to a crisp."

"What?" Her brow furrows before glancing at the flaming marshmallow. "Oh! You distracted me with your dirty talking."

Chuckling, I shake my head. Stirring in the rum, I pour us each a cup of cocoa while she focuses on making us s'mores. A few minutes later, she hands me my s'more and I give her a cup of cocoa. Hugging it with her hands, she blows on it before taking a sip.

Her eyes widen with surprise, looking at me over the rim. "This is really good."

"No faith in me?" I let the delight show in my eyes.

"When you poured in the rum I was a little," she holds her fingers a pinch away from each other, "concerned."

"Surprised you didn't speak up."

"I planned to talk shit if it tasted like trash."

I grin. "That sounds more like you."

"You know me so well already." She smiles.

We sit, eating our s'mores and drinking our cocoa. I have to admit, it's nice to not be alone on this trip. Last year, I went home early because I got tired of the silence and figured I could do the same thing in the comfort of my own home. I didn't invite Noelle to stay with the intention of fucking her. That's just an unexpected pleasure.

She pulls me from my thoughts when she sets her cup down. "Can I try something with you?" There's a glimmer in her eye.

"Yeah," I put the last bite of s'more into my mouth. "What is it?"

"Snow blowing." She smiles, licking her lips, and pulls her braids back into a low ponytail.

11

Noelle

"Is it a game?" He eyes me over the rim of his cup as he finishes his cocoa.

"You can call it that." I reach for the buckle of his belt.

It dawns on him what's about to happen as his eyes widen and he glances over his shoulder. "We're not here alone, you know that, right?"

"That's what makes this fun." This is the only opportunity I have to cross snow blowing off my imaginary list I made up just now. Not that I need a list to have a craving to taste him.

Taking off my gloves, I dip my hand into his pants. He groans when my fingers wrap around his shaft. I'm about to put these snow pants to the test. Getting on my knees, I give him a sultry smile. There's something about the way he's looking down at me that makes me aware of the heartbeat between my legs.

"I've been wanting to do this since yesterday." I pull his dick out of his pants, licking the precum off that's glistening on the tip.

"Shit." He draws out the 's' and I watch his eyes slowly shut. "Don't let me stop you."

Spitting on it, I take him into my mouth, wrapping my hand around the base so I don't choke on him... just yet. I use my hand to jerk him off while I make his shaft glisten with my mouth.

"You look so fucking good with those perfect lips of yours wrapped around me."

I've never been with a man who is as vocal as Snow is during sex. I love the praise. It makes me want to please him. I hold his gaze as I suck on him. Grabbing the waist of his pants, he lifts his hips so I can pull them down further. I use my free hand to massage his balls.

"Fuck," he bites on his lower lip, trying to keep his eyes on me. "That's a good girl. Just like that."

Sucking on him harder, he grabs the ponytail at the base of my neck, wrapping it around his wrist.

"Take it all..." He breathes out, keeping a firm grip on my hair as he pumps into my mouth.

Removing my hand that's around the base of him, I deep throat his length.

"Goddamn." He groans, watching the inches slide in and out of my mouth. "Ah, fuck you, feel amazing."

His head falls back, and I know he's on the cusp of his release. Looking up, I savor the sight of him coming undone for me.

He meets my gaze. "You're going to make me cum, Noelle."

Instead of pulling off, I hollow my cheeks, making him moan as he spills into my mouth. His grip on my hair loosens, and his body relaxes as I drag my lips off the length of him.

Letting go of my hair, he wraps his hand around my throat. "Swallow." He applies light pressure, holding my gaze. "I want you to remember the taste of me."

The ache between my thighs begs for release. Closing my mouth, I swallow his salty, sweet release.

With his hand still around my throat, He pulls me toward him, whispering in my ear. "That's a good girl." Letting go of me, he pulls up his pants, refastening his belt.

"Can you fuck me now?" I ask, still on my knees. Not caring how desperate I sound.

He flashes me a smile, pulling me onto his lap. "I'll do more than that, but unless you'd like an audience, it's probably best we wait until we get back to the cabin."

Chuckling, he bites my bottom lip before kissing me. The sound of the stable door opening pulls me from our moment.

"Fine." I slide off his lap. "I'll wait."

"You're cute when you pout." He wraps his arm around my neck, kissing my temple.

The sled pulls up seconds later. "Did you two enjoy yourselves?"

Snow helps me get in. My body warms, wondering if she saw me bobbing for apples on his dick. "We did." I smile, not meeting her gaze.

"Good. There's a blanket back there if you're cold."

"Thank you." Snow smiles, sitting beside me.

The driver turns back around, signaling the horse to go. Snow pulls me flush against his side, throwing the blanket over our laps. He drapes his arm over my shoulders and slips his other hand underneath the blanket, tugging at the button of my pants.

"Can you keep quiet, Snowflake?" he whispers in my ear, undoing my pants, and slipping his hand into my panties.

"Mhmm," I moan softly, nodding my head yes as he dips his fingers into my wetness.

"Good, because I'm going to make you cum for me. You want to cum for me, right? That's why you were begging on your knees for me to fuck you." I nod my head yes. "No, say it." He cups my chin with his hand that's wrapped around my shoulders, cradling my head as I look up at him.

"Yes, I want to cum for you."

"Open your legs for me." I listen, spreading them open and glancing at the driver. I'm losing my fucking mind as he massages my clit. "Focus on me. Your only job right now is for you to cum."

His fingers soothe the ache between my thighs as he alternates between sinking his fingers into my wetness and teasing my clit.

"Tell me how it feels, Snowflake."

"S-So Good..." I moan louder than I mean to.

He claps his hand over my mouth, whispering, "Gotta keep it down, Snowflake or I won't let you cum."

I whimper into his palm, squeezing my eyes shut. Picking up the pace, he rubs my clit. My breath hitches as heat spreads over my skin. The coiling tension gripping me tighter until it snaps. I free fall into ecstasy, opening like a dam for him.

"Mmm... I love when you cum for me." He mutters into my ear.

He replaces his hand over my mouth with his lips, quieting my moans. My body quakes with pleasure. I forget that we're outside on a sleigh with another person only a few feet from us. I tangle my fingers in his curls, needing something to hold onto. Breaking the kiss, he pulls away. I slowly open my eyes to focus on him.

I'll never be the same after this vacation is over... after Snow's touch.

He slowly slides his fingers out of me, bringing them to his lips, and sucks my release off them. "Is it just me, or do you get sweeter with each orgasm?"

"Dammit, Snow." I rest my head on his arm. "This dirty, sexy talk and the way you feel are making me insatiable."

He chuckles, pressing a kiss to my temple. "When we get back to the cabin, I'll get you cleaned up and properly fucked."

Heat pools between my thighs as if I didn't just cum for him.

After getting back to the cabin yesterday, he did in fact clean me up, and then we only left the bed to eat dinner and fell right back into it. I never remember having a sex drive like this. The only reason I'm out from under Snow right now is because I want to get him a Christmas gift and need to find a printer.

"I'll be back," I say, pulling on my coat.

"You're leaving me?"

"Yes." I lean over the back of the couch, giving him a kiss. "And I'm never coming back."

Grabbing my arms, he pulls me over the back of the couch. I laugh hysterically as I fall into his lap. "Don't let the door hit your ass on the way out."

"Damn. Not even a goodbye?"

"No, because I have something you can't seem to get enough of."

I smile, stretching out on his lap. "Call me a fiend. I don't care. I want it. I need it and I'll fucking have it."

"Yes, you will." He kisses me. "Where are you going anyway?"

"To get your gift."

"Gift? I didn't realize we were – "

"No pressure, Snow." I smooth my hand over his chest. "You don't have to get me anything, but I want to get you something. Why do you look... tense?"

His brow is furrowed with thought. "Because I haven't bought a gift for someone other than family and Wilder in a while."

"Don't feel obligated. I simply wanted to do something for you."

Even if we weren't intimately involved, I'd still want to get him something. Hopefully he wants to remember this trip forever like I do.

I smooth my fingertips over the crease between his brows. "Don't think too hard. I'll be back."

"Alright." He kisses me before I rise to my feet.

Pressing my fingers to my lips, I smile as I leave him on the couch. Everything about him–*us*–feels right. I can respect we're here on vacation, thoroughly enjoying each other, but... I can't help to think beyond the present.

Snow seems like he's still madly in love with his late fiancée. I wonder if he sees me as the second best option. Shit, I wonder if I'm an option or just a release. He did say he's never experienced a connection like ours before.

Blowing out a puff of air, I try to think of something other than Snow. My phone vibrates in my pocket. It's texts in the group chat I have with Aspen and Eve. Smiling, I forgot I posted a picture of Snow. Well sort of, it's his hand holding my chin while I have a cheesy smile on my face. I took a few photos of us while we were lying in bed earlier.

Aspen: Bitch! Whose sexy ass hand is on you like you're theirs?
Eve: And she said she wasn't there for dick.
Elle: A friend's...

Aspen: With benefits?
Elle: Lots of them.
Eve: The biggest heaux of us all.
**Aspen: And you post only a sneak peek of him? I know Malcolm
is crying, screaming, and throwing up like the punk ass bitch he
is.**
Elle: He's not concerned with me.

We're not even friends on social media anymore. The only way he'd
see what I'm up to is if I were tagged in a mutual friend's photo. I am
still friends with his sister though, but I can't imagine her going out of
her way to – actually... yes she would. She's petty and thought I was too
good for Malcolm.

Eve: I'll make sure he sees it.
Elle: Let me have my peace.
Eve: Have all the peace you want. He cannot.

I'm sure I look insane, cackling by myself on the way to the lobby.

Aspen: Send us a picture of mystery man's face.
Elle: No.

I want to keep Snow to myself for a little while longer. Plus, I don't
know if we'll last past these next few days. I laugh at myself, saying 'we'
as if we are something.

Eve: Greedy bitch.

Elle: Also, cross snow blowing off my life's bucket list please.
Eve: I KNEW IT!!!! You're getting your back cracked out there.
Aspen: What is snow blowing???
Elle: Love you guys. Text later.

Exiting the chat, I slide my phone in my pocket as I walk through the lobby doors. I smile at Nicholas behind the counter.

"Just the man I want to see. Hi, Nicholas."

"Miss Frost. How was your sleigh ride yesterday?"

"Good!" I hope the embarrassment doesn't show on my face. My body tingles with the memories.

"Wonderful. What can I help you with today?"

"Is there a printer around here that I could use to print off some pictures?"

"You can use the office printer if you like? We use it to print off photos for the resort."

"That would be perfect. Thank you."

"Right this way." He holds the door open on the side of the counter for me.

I follow him behind the desk and down the short hallway. At the end of it, he enters a nicely decorated office.

"The printer is wireless. You can connect your phone to it and print the pictures that way you're not having to upload anything onto the computer."

"Thank you so much, Nicholas."

He helps me find the printer on my phone and then leaves me to sort through the pictures. I'm grateful I didn't have to upload them to a computer. Some of them are risqué, but I wanted Snow to have a physical reminder of the memories we've created together.

I print off the picture of us feeding reindeer, hoping he always remembers that sense of wonder. Scrolling to the picture of us with our reindeer cookies makes me laugh. I have to give him this one too. He knew good and damn well he was going to win, but he let me talk my shit and then reaped the benefits. I choose a couple of me running through the snow with my ass out. It's the first time I've looked at them and my cheeks hurt from smiling so hard. I get to one that makes me laugh so loud, I clap my hand over my mouth.

Snow has me flipped over his shoulder, ass on full display, arms out to the side, and he's smiling nonchalantly. He must've taken it while he was threatening my life with hypothermia. The next one is of us together in bed the morning after we first hooked up. The post sex glow is real. He is delectable. Looking at the picture of him makes me squeeze my thighs together. Scrolling further, I choose a few more from the sleigh ride and this morning. It ends up being ten pictures in total. Once I figure out the sizing, it takes me no time to print them off. Now I just need to find some frames.

Coming out of the back room, Nicholas is in the middle of helping someone. Rounding the front desk, I wait until he's done to see if he can suggest a shop that sells frames that won't cost me a year's worth of rent. The gift shops here are cute, but as in any tourist location, insanely overpriced.

"Did you get the pictures you needed?"

"Yes, now I just need frames or something similar… that won't cost me an arm and a leg."

He chuckles. "I understand. There's a gift shop called Nightingale just up the road. They sell reasonably priced gift items."

"You're the best, Nicholas. Thank you. Oh, and Merry Christmas."

"Merry Christmas, Miss Frost. Will you be at the ball tomorrow?"

"Wouldn't miss it." I smile, walking out the door.

SNOW

Walking to the market, I pull out my phone and call Winter.

"Didn't expect to hear your voice for a few more days." He answers.

"Yeah, well, I need some advice." I cut to the chase.

"From... *me*?"

Winter is my big brother, and after everything, I still look up to him.

"Why do you sound surprised?"

"It's just... are you sure you want advice from me?"

He may spend most of his time in bed with women, but he's also a romantic. Winter wasn't always a playboy. He didn't make meaningless sex his life's mission until after our dad died. Before he fell off the deep end for a while, he was hopelessly devoted to a woman he was set to marry. That fell apart when he did.

"I wouldn't have bothered calling if I didn't. Anyway," I let out a long, low sigh. "It's been a while since I've thought about anyone else... romantically. I met someone here, and I'd like to get her a Christmas gift, but I don't know what. I'm not even sure I'll see her again after this. But I want it to matter."

"Make it memorable. What can you get her to remind her of you?"

Winter is easy to talk to because he doesn't need every detail to help.

"A diamond necklace and earrings won't cut it?" I ask jokingly.

"That's bullshit anyone can buy. It doesn't have any sentimental value. Unless she's into that shit, but I doubt you'd be into someone who's materialistic."

He's right. Noelle isn't materialistic. She's down to earth and would rather have a good story to tell instead of something to show for it. An idea comes to me as I near the market street.

"Can I ask why you think you won't see her after this?"

I stop in my tracks, rubbing the back of my neck. "I'm not sure I'm ready... you know? It's not fair to expect something with her when I'm still thinking of Kenna."

Noelle deserves everything. Not fragments.

"I respect that..."

"But?" I coax him.

"But... have you ever thought, just maybe, Kenna wasn't the one? Not saying that Miss Mistletoe Mountain is – " I chuckle at the name he's given her " – but maybe it's time you open up to the possibility of more. It's not so much about someone being better for you as it is about someone who your soul recognizes."

"And you wonder why I ask you for advice?" He chuckles. I'm silent for a few breaths before I ask, "You still miss her, don't you?"

"Every fucking waking moment." I hear the pain in his words without having to see it etched on his face.

"Maybe you two will find your way back to each other."

He scoffs. "I fucking doubt it. I saw her recently. Even from across the room I recognized her energy."

"And you didn't say anything?"

"Fuck no!" He shouts, making me laugh. "Got the fuck outta there before she saw me."

"It'd be crazy if you, I don't know, actually talked to her."

"I like my balls. Thank you."

We laugh together. "I'm going to see if I can find a gift. Thanks for bringing me back to earth."

"Always here to humble you." He pauses before speaking again. "Moving on doesn't mean you loved Kenna any less. Appreciate what you two did have, but don't be a prisoner to the past like I am, Snow."

"Yeah..." I continue down the snow covered path. "Love you, Winter. I'll talk to you tomorrow."

"Love you too, bro. Have fun jingling your balls."

I scoff, laughing. "Fuck off. Bye."

Ending the call, I slide my phone into my pocket, hoping I can find a gift for Noelle.

A few hours later, I arrive back at the cabin and smile when I see Noelle sitting on the counter flipping through a menu. Looking up, she eyes the bags in my hands, smiling.

"No pressure, Snow. You don't have to get me anything." I reiterate her words from earlier.

Hopping off the counter, she laughs. "I didn't want you to feel pressured, but I was secretly hoping you would get me something."

I may be romantically out of touch, but I'm not an idiot. "I can pick up on hints."

"Speaking of hints," She follows behind me to the Christmas tree, watching me place the presents underneath it. "Can I – "

"No. How are you going to want a gift, but then want to know what it is?"

She snorts with laughter. "You didn't even let me ask my question!"

"The answer is still no." I straighten up, turning to face her.

"Fine." Rolling her eyes, she smiles. "It's Christmas Eve. What do you want to do?"

"Do you want to go to dinner?" She gapes at me. "What?"

"Just days ago you were about to puke by the mere thought of asking me to dinner. You just asked me so effortlessly!"

"Formalities are out the window now with the way I've stayed buried inside you."

"Oh," She puts her hands on her hips, nodding her head. "You just had to fuck me? Makes total sense."

I smile, grabbing her, and pulling her into me. "No, that's not what I meant. I'm comfortable with you now."

"I know what you meant." She wraps her arms around my middle. "But I wanted to be a smartass."

"You," I smack her ass, she lets out a mix of a moan and yelp. "Are a smartass. Now," I kiss her neck. "Can I take you to dinner, please?"

"Yes." She presses a kiss to my lips, grabbing my hand and pulling me toward the bedroom.

It's no surprise that I'm ready before she is, but when Noelle reappears, I realize I'd easily wait as long as she needed me to. She's wearing a short red satin skirt with thigh high black velvet heeled boots, and a cream colored sweater. I immediately picture her skirt hiked up her waist with her legs wrapped around me.

"Are we going to make it out of the cabin?" She gives me a brilliant smile as she puts on an earring.

Licking my lips, I consider taking her back to bed. "We both need sustenance. Then we can play."

"You look handsome." Her eyes rake over my body. "I'm surprised you packed something festive."

Smoothing my hand over my cranberry red sweater, I smile. "I didn't. Picked it up while buying your gifts along with something for the ball tomorrow."

Her whole being lights up as she bounces with excitement. "You're going with me?!"

"No. Some other woman I met while shopping."

She playfully shoves my arm. "I thought you said you weren't going."

"I hadn't planned on it until I saw how excited you were, so I guess I'll suffer through."

"This makes me happy." She grins. "I didn't want to spend my last night here without you."

A mix of emotions flood me. Tomorrow is our last day together. We'll be back to reality soon. I wonder if we'll exist outside of the world we've created here. These past few days with her have felt like a lifetime.

"Ready?" She pulls on her wool coat.

"Yeah." I respond, focusing on her.

She slips her hand into mine as we walk out the door.

Noelle laughs hysterically as I carry her back to the cabin. I'm doing the song 'Last Christmas' by Wham! no justice as I sing it at the top of my lungs. She wheezes with laughter when I forget the lyrics, stumbling through, until I get to the chorus.

"Sing it, baby!" She shouts, kicking a foot up into the air.

She joins in singing, no better than me, as we sing the last lines in unison. I fall into laughter with her.

"You cannot tell me that's not one of *thee* best Christmas songs of all time." She says, sucking on a candy cane.

We both had a few drinks and are a little tipsy.

"It's definitely in the top three for the beat alone." I reassure her.

"'Santa Baby' sung by Eartha Kitt will always be number one for me."

"Fuck, that's a good one. Her voice is phenomenal. I'm adding that to my top three too."

"What's another one?" She rests her head on my shoulder.

"You're about to talk so much shit, but "You're a Mean One, Mr. Grinch" is one of my childhood favorites."

Lifting her head, she bites her lip, trying to hold it in, but tosses her head back, howling with laughter.

"Talk your shit. I don't care. It will forever be one of my favorites."

"The Grinch?" She catches her breath. "That really is so cute though. I'm not even gonna lie, that song is a banger." She rattles off some of the lyrics, making me smile.

"Damn right it is."

"We have impeccable taste, Mr. King."

"Indeed, Miss Frost."

She smiles, resting her head on my shoulder again. "Thank you for carrying me back to the cabin."

"Couldn't have you injuring yourself, trying to walk on those stilts." I eye her heels.

It was snowing when we left for dinner. By the time we ate, had a few drinks, and danced a little the snow fall became heavier. Now I'm carrying her through calf deep snow.

"You have to admit, I do look sexy." She holds up her foot, turning it side to side.

"That's always been a fact, Snowflake."

"You like me even after I pepper sprayed you? I was so afraid you hated me."

"I was rightfully angry." She laughs softly. "But hating you never crossed my mind. So, yes, I like you." *A lot more than I should* I say to myself.

"Good." She kisses my neck. "I like you a lot too."

The cabin comes in view through the dense snow fall. I'm silent, repeating her words in my head. Does that mean we're feeling the same thing?

Reaching the cabin, I cautiously walk up the steps. Glancing at Noelle, her eyes are closed.

"Noelle..."

"Hmm?" She hums with her eyes closed.

"The key."

She pulls it from her jacket pocket, handing it to me. Once we're inside, I set her down on her feet. Sitting on the bench, I slide off my snow covered boots and then take off my pants that have snow clinging to the bottom half. Noelle makes her way to the couch, collapsing onto it. Before I join her, I grab some sweats from my suitcase.

"Are you sleeping?" I kneel beside her.

"Uh uh."

"I have a gift for you."

Her eyes snap open. "For me to open now?"

"Well now I know how to wake you up." I chuckle.

Grabbing the gift from under the tree, I hand it to her as she sits up.

"Did you wrap this?" She smiles.

"Am I not Martha Stewart's protégé?"

She giggles. "Damn, I paid someone to wrap yours."

"Remember who my parents are. Wrapping gifts was serious business. I could do it in my sleep."

"Yeah, yeah. No need to brag." She fakes annoyance.

She pulls at the crimson ribbon, carefully untying it. Then she tears through the paper like Edward Scissorhands. I laugh indulgently, watching her. She tosses the box's top aside and looks at me before pulling out what's in the box.

Her eyes widen. "Silk pajamas!" She rubs the material between her fingers.

"Just so you know, I looked in your suitcase for your size." Giving me a wave of her hand, she brushes away my admission.

Inspecting them, she squeals. "The snowflake embroidered on the pocket! This is – " Pulling out the rest, she grins, pointing at the pocket of my set that has a reindeer on it. "You got us matching sets?"

"Yes." I smile at her joy.

"I'll never forget you fucking swindling me."

"I loved your false confidence. Worked in my favor."

"Snow..." Her lips turn downward, giving me a sympathetic look. "This is such a thoughtful gift." Getting up, she wraps her arms around me. "Thank you."

"You're welcome, Snowflake." I give her a tight hug, pressing a kiss to her forehead.

"Now, we have to change into these and take pictures by the tree." She smiles, looking up at me.

"Let's do it." I pick up my set.

After pictures, we settle on the couch in front of the fire. We lie body to body, limbs tangled, with a blanket draped over us. The only light is the warm glow of the flames with Christmas songs playing softly in the background.

"Merry Christmas, Snow," she mutters as her eyes close.

"Merry Christmas, Noelle." I kiss her cheek.

Holding her in my arms, I hope this isn't my last Christmas with her.

12
SNOW

"I CAN'T BELIEVE THEY had to cancel the ball." Noelle whines with a forlorn expression, looking out the window as we finish up lunch.

We received alerts earlier this morning that they're dealing with frozen pipes in the building where the ball was supposed to be held. It flooded and ruined some of the décor. I'm not surprised. We woke up to a drift of snow up to my knees and it's still in the negatives now at noon. There isn't another space large enough for the people who were planning to attend. Needless to say, Noelle was dramatically devastated when she received the news that there wasn't another area for the ball to be held. Call me a grinch, but I'd rather spend our last night together alone in the cabin than drinking and dancing.

"We still have our gift exchange."

She perks up, momentarily forgetting about the canceled ball. "That's right!" Finishing the food on her plate, she sets her fork aside. "I'm ready."

Getting up from the table, I take her hand, leading her toward the tree. We sit beside it on a plush fur rug in our matching pajamas. It's been years since I celebrated Christmas. I forgot the anticipation that settles in the night before and morning of.

Reaching under the tree, I hold her gift in my hands, looking at the glittery gold bow. "This time with you has been incredible. I think the grinch would say his heart grew, but mine... I'm pretty sure the heat of the pepper spray – " she laughs " – and your heart of gold thawed it out, making me feel alive again."

Her beautiful brown eyes become glossy. She gives me a hug before tearing into the present. Her hands slow as she lifts the top off the box.

"Snow..." She gasps, pulling out the necklace. "This is gorgeous." The necklace glints and gleams as she holds it up. "Look at the little charms!" She grins.

I watch her inspect the diamond encrusted snowflake and reindeer hanging from the dainty gold chain. After looking through shops for longer than I cared to, this is the only thing I found that I felt would be meaningful to her.

"Are these real diamonds?"

My brows knit together. "What else would they be?"

"I don't know Swarovski crystals or something." She moves the charms back and forth, making them catch the light.

"Swarovski?" I can't help the look of disgust on my face.

She splays her hand across her chest. "Excuse me, Daddy Warbucks!"

"I'm sorry." I laugh at her Annie joke. "Sometimes I can't hide my emotions."

"No, it's fine. I love that about you."

Love? My mind goes into overdrive. She loves something about me? "You told me I had RBF. Now I can't hide my emotions. Which is it?"

"You're stoic until you're comfortable, but you can have RBF even if you can't hide your emotions. But I ask because I don't want you putting yourself out for me. I don't care about money, but I also don't know how deep your pockets – "

"Bottomless." Her eyes snap to mine. "Whatever I give you is always going to be real, Snowflake."

She holds my gaze, before looking at the necklace in her hands again. "Can you put it on me, please?"

"I'd love to."

Taking the necklace from her hands, I sit beside her. She pulls her hair up, and I wrap it around her neck. My fingertips brush against her skin, causing goosebumps to appear. I love knowing I have this effect on her. Fastening her necklace, I adjust it, and then press a kiss to her neck.

"Perfect," I mutter against her skin.

Noelle

A shiver ripples through me as his lips meet my skin. I smile as I hear him breathe the word "perfect". I look down at the charms adorning my neck. The snowflake is encrusted in white diamonds. The reindeer has brown for the face, yellow for the antlers, and black diamonds for the eyes with a red one for the nose. It's thoughtful and perfect.

Turning to face him, I press a kiss to his lips. "Thank you."

"You're welcome. Now, where's my gift?" He flashes me a brilliant smile.

"No patience." My heart drums against my chest. I hope he doesn't think it's ridiculous. Pulling it out from under the tree, I hand it to him.

"This feels heavy." He moves it up and down as if his hands are a scale.

"It's a years' worth of pepper spray." I smile sweetly, batting my lashes.

He smirks. "Half of your supply then?"

Before I can respond, he starts tearing through the wrapping paper. My palms sweat as he reveals the bright red box. I watch as he takes off the top, removing the gold tissue paper, and peers at the photos beneath it. He pauses, staring at the pictures. They're held in simple silver 4x6 frames. Pulling each one out, he pauses when he gets to the one of me over his shoulder and he grins. It's the only fancy frame with snowflake details engraved in it.

"These pictures are amazing," he says, looking through them again.

"I wanted you to remember me... us and our time here."

"I couldn't forget you even if I wanted to."

I could blame what I feel for Snow on our close proximity or his attractiveness. He's striking, but I gravitate to him because of his personality. Beneath his stoic expression and hard exterior is a thoughtful and caring man.

"I was worried you wouldn't like it."

"I love it." He looks at me, pulling me into him, and presses a kiss to my temple. "Thank you." I squeeze him tight before he pulls away, picking up the picture of him carrying me over his shoulder. "This one is going in my room."

"Not on your desk at work?" I smile coyly.

"I don't share, Snowflake." Four simple words have me ready to climb on top of him. He puts the top back on the box, pressing a kiss to my lips. "Thank you for making Christmas feel like magic again."

His words warm me to my core. This is definitely beyond attraction.

"What about the ball were you looking forward to?"

"Dressing up." I smile. "And dancing."

"Then how bout me," he slides closer, "and you," he wraps his arm around my waist, "make that happen." He trails kisses along my collar bone and up my neck.

The feel of his lips make it hard to focus on his words. "I – what did you say?"

He chuckles. "We can have our own, private ball."

"We can do whatever you want." I pull him on top of me, falling back on the couch. "But right now, I want you inside me."

"Greedy little thing," he mutters against my lips, using his other hand to untie the bow at the waist of my pants.

"For you," I breathe.

He smirks, slipping his hand into my pants, giving me what I want. I hum with pleasure as he massages my clit, bringing me to the edge of a climax before he stops. Sitting up, he grabs the waistband of my pants. I lift my hips, letting him drag them off.

"I like to watch you take it while you come undone for me."

As if I needed anymore reason to be a puddle for him. He unbuttons his shirt, taking it off, and his pants quickly follow. I drink him in. Hovering over me, he holds his thick length in his hands, stroking himself. I wrap my hand around his, guiding him to the pool of wetness between my thighs. Snow needs no guidance, swiftly burying himself to the hilt. I drape one leg over the back of the couch and he grips the other in his hand, spreading me open for him.

Moans spill from my lips with each jolt of pleasure the thrusts of his hips gives. He rubs my clit, making my eyes roll back.

"This is what you wanted?"

"Mmhmm..." I moan, biting my lip. Him, filling me up and being in his space is a need now. Not just want.

"Look at you take it like such a good girl... fucking beautiful..."

His eyes trail over my body, admiring every inch. I've never felt worshipped like I do under the gaze of Snow King. Our eyes lock, and it's my destruction. I fall into a euphoric oblivion as he plunges into me, taking everything.

He falls with me seconds later, filling me with his warmth. His hips slowly stutter to a halt. With him lying on top of me, chest to chest, I wrap my legs and arms around him. I feel his heart pounding against mine as we come down from our high.

"Can I ask you a question?"

He props himself up on his elbows, looking at me. "Anything."

"Why did you let me stay with you?"

"I didn't let you, I *wanted* you to stay."

"Why?" My brows knit together.

"Because you're gorgeous, and I wanted your company."

I blink, giggling. "That's it?"

"Yeah." He grins. "Hopefully you weren't expecting some poetic response."

"I didn't know what to expect, but it wasn't that."

"As annoying as you were, Snowflake," he presses a kiss to my forehead. "There was no way I could deny your beauty. Not with those brown eyes."

"They're just brown..." I look off to the side briefly before meeting his gaze.

"They've given me a glimpse of light that I haven't seen in a long fucking time. So, no," he holds my gaze. "They're not just brown."

His words fill me to the brim with happiness as I wrap my arms tightly around him.

Later that evening, I'm getting ready to go to dinner with Snow, still feeling disappointed about the ball being canceled. At least the snow has stopped falling outside so we won't have to trudge through it to get to the restaurant. Coming out of the bathroom, rubbing the last bit of lotion into my skin, I eye the gold dress glinting in the light. It's a little over the top for dinner, but I refuse to let it go to waste. Pulling it on, it's floor length, flaring slightly at the bottom, as the rest clings to my curves. The necklace Snow gave me matches it perfectly. I admire myself in the mirror, knowing, and loving, that Snow is going to eat me up in this dress.

The thought makes me smile as I apply a deep crimson lipstick. Slipping into some strappy black heels, I give myself one last look in the mirror. Walking out to meet Snow, I stop in my tracks at the scene before me. He's transformed the dining area into an elegant setting with candles and décor. Christmas music is playing softly in the background.

Meeting my gaze, he smiles as he saunters toward me. "I'm going to be honest, Snowflake..." He wraps his arm around my waist. "This is our last night, and I wanted you all to myself."

"Ah," I smile up at him. "Did you sabotage the ballroom?"

A chuckle resonates in his chest. "No, that was the universe giving me what I want."

"And what's that?"

"You."

His words wash over me as he presses a soft kiss to my lips. "Shall we eat?"

"Yes," I say, letting him guide me toward the table.

I've had boyfriends, Malcolm being the longest relationship, and not one of them showed up for me the way Snow has. The simple things like this cause feelings beyond like to bud.

"This is amazing, Snow." I sit as he pulls the chair out for me.

He removes the dome off of my plate, revealing braised short ribs that make my mouth water. Taking a seat, he splays his napkin across his lap.

"You look stunning." He pours us wine.

"Thank you." I smile, grabbing my glass, and taking a sip.

"Pleasure is all mine."

I don't know that I can handle going back to reality as if we never happened.

"Is this it for us?" The question falls from my lips before I can stop myself.

We both came here, tending broken hearts. It's probably not the best dynamic, but I can't deny what I feel for him past the physical connection.

Setting his glass aside, he meets my gaze. "I hope we can see what happens with us outside of this cabin when we get back home."

"You want... more?"

He's silent for a moment, focusing on the candles flame. "Time with you has helped me catch a glimpse of myself that I buried underneath the grief. You remind me that life's worth living."

My nose stings as tears pool in my eyes.

He grabs my hand, tracing small circles with his thumb. "Can we continue to get to know each other when we get back to Hope Valley?"

"I'd love that." I smile.

Taking things slow isn't a bad idea. I didn't expect him to become my boyfriend. I'm not sure I want to deep dive into another relationship right now. We may get back to Hope Valley and the spark we feel here, in one another's gravity, could dwindle as we return to our daily lives.

"Have you had other romantic relationships... since Kenna?" I take a bite of the delicious braised short ribs to give myself something to do.

"Not romantic." He wipes his mouth with his napkin. "I've had other sexual partners, trying to fill a void." I try not to let the disappointment show, but he picks up on it and grabs my hand, making me look at him. "That's not what we've been. You are the exception, Snowflake."

I know we happened fast. In the past, it's taken me awhile to get comfortable with someone before sleeping with them. With Snow, I *crave* to fall into bed with him. Even if he did tell me I was filling a void, it would sting, but I wouldn't regret the experience of him. The look in his eyes as he kisses the back of my hand conveys *I am* the exception. The doubt that momentarily creeped in dissipates. We continue talking, eating, and laughing until our plates are clean and half the wine bottle is gone.

Clasping my hands together under my chin, I smile at him. "I have to admit... being with you is better than going to a ball."

He smiles, rising to his feet, and holds his hand out to me. "Say that again, Snowflake."

I place my hand in his, letting out a laugh. "Again, arrogance is a trait you could've kept hidden."

"And hide all my good parts?" He glances at his watch, pulling me along behind him. "I think not."

"Where are you taking me?"

"It's a surprise. You'll need a jacket." He glances at my heels. "And your Moon Boots."

I gasp dramatically. "You *want* me to wear them?"

"I don't want you to freeze."

"Mhmm." I smile coyly. "I think you like them."

"Get your atrocious boots and jacket."

"Alright, alright!" I laugh, sitting on the bench near the door to put on my boots. Tightening them around my calves, I ask, "Where are we going?"

"I just want to show you something."

I eye him suspiciously, pulling on my jacket. "Okay..."

"Just trust me." He smiles brilliantly.

"I'm ready to be surprised." I stand in front of him.

"Close your eyes and keep them closed, okay?"

I nod my head, closing them, and he grabs my hand. Cold air momentarily steals my breath when he opens the door.

"Watch your step," he says, guiding me off the porch.

Snow crunches beneath our feet as he leads me into the night. The quiet that settles over the mountain at night brings a peace I haven't felt elsewhere. It could also be Snow's warm palm in mine. We walk in silence, me with my eyes closed, for a few minutes. If he didn't tell me where we were going back at the cabin, I doubt he'd tell me now. His steps stop eventually, and I keep walking cautiously as he pulls me in front of him. I feel his hands on my waist and his chest to my back.

"Look up, Snowflake," he whispers in my ear.

Listening, my eyes meet ribbons of color rippling across the sky. I've never seen anything as enchanting as the bluish green currents of light dancing through the stars. I feel Snow slip his hand into mine, interlacing our fingers.

Everything ceases to exist except for me and him, hand in hand, in this moment.

I'm speechless, captivated by the ribbons of lights above us. Tears prick my eyes. I don't bother trying to swipe them away because sharing this moment with him is one of the best of my life. We stand in silence, staring at the lights until they become faint. I blink, becoming aware of the cold seeping into my bones and how my face is getting numb.

"Snow..." I'm still at a loss for words as I turn to face him.

"I wanted you to see the northern lights."

"That was..." I glance up at the barely visible streaks of light. "Enthralling," is the only word I can think of.

"Interesting," he says glancing at my lips. "That's the word I'd use to describe you."

Wrapping my arms around his neck, I pull him toward me until our lips meet. He deepens the kiss, slipping his tongue into my mouth. This moment and the way he feels has me in a state of bliss.

Pulling away, he rests his forehead against mine. "I think we should take this back to the cabin so we don't freeze."

"You could take me against that tree right now, and I wouldn't – "

Picking me up, he wraps my legs around his waist. I hear the seam of my dress rip against the pressure of me spreading my legs for him. He presses me up against the tree, and I feel the throbbing anticipation in my center.

"I hope your words are true, Snowflake." He hikes my dress up around my hips. "Because all I need is your permission."

"Take me..."

He makes quick work of unbuttoning his pants. Pulling my panties to the side, he buries himself inside me. My eyes roll back with the jolt of pleasure. He groans, thrusting into me with wild abandon. He wraps his hand around my throat, bringing my gaze back to him. The intense look of desire in his eyes is electric. He hooks his arms underneath my legs, gripping my ass, spreading me wide open for him. The angle lets him plunge deeper and the friction of his thrusts against my clit have me teetering on the edge.

"Mmm... I can feel your pussy tightening. You're going to cum for me aren't you?"

"Yes..." I moan.

"I want you to come on my dick like a good girl. Are you a good girl?"

"I'm a good girl..."

"Yes, you are. You're my good girl."

"Shit..." I hiss as I unravel for him, wrapping my arms tightly around his neck.

"Give it to me." His thrusts become deeper, carrying me into ecstasy.

This is the most connected I've felt to someone during sex. It's as if there's a string, tethering us to one another. The intense orgasm flows through me like the lights in the sky.

"Fuck..." He grunts, his warmth filling me seconds later.

When his thrusts slow, he unhooks my legs from his arms, letting my feet touch the ground. He presses a kiss to my lips, and I savor it.

"Noelle..." He rests his forehead against mine. "I think you were made for me."

I look up at him, lips slightly parted, as his words take up residence in my soul. Made... for him? I've heard sentiments from lovers before, but nothing compares to Snow's words.

"C'mon," he says before I can respond. Not that I could find the words even if I wanted to. Adjusting my jacket, he scoops me into his arms. "Let's get back to the cabin so I can have you again."

13
SNOW

FOR THE FIRST TIME ever, I'm disappointed to see the sun rise. We leave today. I'm anticipating the bubble we've been in bursting. It's my automatic response to anything good coming my way. I've learned to be cautious when things feel they can't get any better. What could possibly be better than Noelle?

I kept good on my word and had her every single way I could last night. Eventually, we fell asleep naked, wrapped up in each other, on the fur rug in front of the fire. I finally feel like I'm living and not simply existing. For five years, I felt stuck under a fog. Then I met Noelle.

My alarm on my phone trills from somewhere in the cabin. I'm cursing myself for setting up such an early flight. Noelle stirs, squinting at the sun's rays filling the living room.

"Turn it off," she groans. "Who gets up at this ungodly hour?"

Chuckling, I wrap her up in my arms. "Me, Snowflake. I leave in a few hours."

Her eyes snap open. "We go home today!"

"Unfortunately..." I mutter.

"What time is your flight?"

"Nine. Yours?"

"Two." She laughs softly. "Check out isn't until eleven. I wanted to be sure to enjoy every minute."

"Did you?"

She lifts her head enough to look at me. "Of course. You were here."

"I know. I just wanted to hear you say it."

Her laughter fills the air. "You call me annoying."

"You are."

"That would be believable if you hadn't feasted on my pussy all night."

"You taste good. Give my compliments to the chef." She laughs softly. "If I didn't have to pack, get ready, and catch a flight, I'd eat you for breakfast."

She lets out an exasperated sigh. "Don't remind me."

Neither of us make a move to get up. We live in the same city, but that's not enough. I want to be in every space she occupies.

"Would you want to fly home with me?" I ask hesitantly.

She sits up, wrapping herself in the blanket. "I think it's a little late to change my flight around. We can – "

"I meant on my jet."

"Yeah, I know. I doubt I'll be able to switch to your flight, let alone sit next to each other."

"Nah, I meant on my private jet."

"Private jet?" Her eyebrows raise, giving me a stunned look.

"Yes. Although you don't have to fly back with me. Only wanted to offer." She may want to fly alone, and I can begrudgingly accept that.

She blinks away the shock. "I'll fly with you. I'm going to be honest, I thought you meant get a seat beside one another, not a whole plane."

I give her a look of amusement. "You don't hide your emotions well either."

"Who casually mentions they have a private jet?" She splays her hand across her chest.

"How else am I supposed to mention it?" I smirk.

She laughs softly. "Good point. What time is it?" She glances around for her phone.

"Six," I say, glancing at my watch. "We have to leave here in an hour because we still have to go through security."

She gives me a bright smile. "Cannot believe I'm getting on a private jet with you. That's something I never thought I'd do."

"I told you everything will always be real with me, Noelle."

After a shower that turned into a sex session, we're scrambling to pack our things. Well... Noelle is scrambling. I'm already done packing and am now handing her stuff I find scattered around the room.

"How do you find anything?" I ask, picking up one of her t-shirts from the floor.

"It's called organized chaos."

"I see the chaos. Organization is a bit of a stretch though."

She stops, glaring up at me. "Maybe if you kept your hands to yourself, I wouldn't be running around like this."

"Oh, I'm sorry. Did you not enjoy yourself?"

She ties her hair back, throwing her toiletry bag into the suitcase. "That's not the point."

I bite my lip, trying to hold back a smile. "It's not?"

Laughing, she shakes her head. "Fuck off, Snow."

"And leave you in your organized chaos alone?" I pick up another clothing item, folding it, and putting it in her suitcase. "You can be the chaos, and I'll be organized."

"I like the sound of that." She smiles.

An hour later, we're walking up the steps to the jet. Rowan, the pilot, greets us as we walk through the door.

"Miss Frost." He smiles. "Pleasure to have you on board."

"Thank you." She smiles, glancing back at me.

"Mr. King, how was your vacation?"

"Good, Rowan. Thank you for asking. How was your Christmas?"

"Really nice." He smiles. "Charlotte said to tell you hello and that you're always welcome to stop by for dinner."

My brothers and I used to get together with Rowan's family all the time. Winter and North go to their house for dinner still. I stopped when Kenna passed and haven't tried since, even though Rowan and Charlotte are always inviting me. He's been our pilot for the past ten years and is more like family.

"I'd love that." I smile at the shocked expression of my acceptance on his face.

"Perfect. Charlotte will be elated. I've got to get ready for takeoff. Enjoy your flight." He smiles, disappearing into the cockpit.

Noelle turns on the spot, taking in everything. "You know, I could get used to this."

I let out a hearty laugh. "Does that mean you'll come back to my place?"

She stops looking around, focusing on me. "You want me to go to your place?"

I furrow my brow. "Isn't that what I just asked?"

"Yes, but – yeah, I'll go with you. Can we stop by my place first so I can change into something else?"

Excitement washes over me at the thought of going to her place. "Of course."

She smiles, turning around, and heads toward the seats. "There's a couch?!"

"Yeah, it turns into a bed for longer flights."

"A bed?" She shoots me a look over her shoulder. "Can it be used for... other activities?"

"Don't tempt me, Snowflake." I tuck a loose braid behind her ear. "You know I have no problem taking you down whenever, wherever."

"I know." She smiles, taking a seat. "And I enjoy it."

Jade, the flight attendant, appears before I can respond. "Good Morning, Mr. King and Miss Frost. My name is Jade, and I'll be your attendant this flight. We're five minutes from takeoff."

"Thank you, Jade," I say before she nods, walking away. I turn my attention back to Noelle. She's resting her head against the seat, staring out the window. "Tired?"

"A little. Now that I'm slowing down."

"We did a lot this week." I smile, thinking of all that we did together.

"Best Christmas ever." She grins, closing her eyes.

"I'm going to have to agree with that."

Opening her eyes, she focuses on me. "This really was your best Christmas?"

"It was," I say without hesitation.

She places her hand over her heart, smiling with tears glistening in her eyes. "Snow... that makes me so happy."

I'm sure she'd hug me if we didn't have our seatbelts on, cruising down the runway for takeoff.

"Noelle..." I smile, looking down at my hands.

"I know. I'm crying, but for you to feel that way after being such a grinch."

I chuckle. "Here I thought we were having a sentimental moment."

"We are." She grins. "I know it isn't easy for you, but I'm glad your best Christmas was with me."

I hold her gaze before she looks out the window, getting the last glimpse of Mistletoe Mountain as we take off. Truth is, she made it easy. I was content with continuing on as I was, accustomed to being alone. Then Noelle lit up my world in vivid color like the northern lights in the sky last night.

Once we're in the air, Rowan alerts us that it's safe to move around the cabin. Jade appears a few moments later.

"Is there anything that either of you need?" She smiles between the two of us.

"Do you have blankets?" Noelle asks.

"Of course. We also have food, drinks, and alcoholic beverages."

"Fruit?" Noelle raises her brows.

"Yes. Fresh fruit." Jade smiles.

"Mimosas?" She tilts her head to the side.

"Those too."

"I'm never going back to flying coach," Noelle says jokingly.

Jade surprises me when she laughs. She had a fling with Winter that ended badly, and she's been rightfully stand offish since. North and I warned him about stringing her along, however, Winter has a knack for doing whatever the hell he wants. After things ended, she wanted to quit, but North and I talked her into continuing flying with us. We left it up to Winter to find his own flight attendant. Eventually, he wisely chose a male. This is the first flight since their falling out that I've seen her truly relaxed and enjoying herself like she used too. Noelle has a way about her that makes others comfortable in her presence.

"And you, Mr. King?"

"Coffee, please."

Jade nods, smiling. "I'll be back in a few moments."

Noelle unbuckles her seatbelt and sits on my lap, holding up her phone. "Smile." Wrapping my arm around her waist, I rest my head on her chest and smile. She takes a few before she's satisfied. "Aw, we look so cute. Do you mind if I post it?"

"No."

"What's your handle? I'll tag you."

"Handle?"

"Yeah. For Instagram."

"I don't have one."

She gapes at me, giving me a look of disbelief. "What?"

"What am I going to show? My depression?"

She tosses her head back, cackling. "If it's any consolation, you wear it well. I'd follow you."

I smile, watching her laugh. "How do I make one?"

"Really?" She quirks a brow. "You want one?"

"Yeah. Why not? Winter and North are always bugging me to get on social media."

Holding out her hand, she says, "Let me see your phone."

We spend the next few minutes making me an Instagram. She also makes me a TikTok to send me funny videos. I watch her post the picture of us to my account. Winter, who is always on social media, comments instantaneously.

Noelle squints at the screen, smiling. "Did he just call me Miss Mistletoe Mountain?"

I chuckle. "Yes, I called him Christmas Eve, and we talked about you. He's... something else." She clicks on his profile, scrolling through pictures. After a few of them, her hand stills as she stares at a picture of him. "Something wrong?"

"Nope." She scrolls through a few more pictures, covering her mouth with her hand. "This is your brother?"

"Yes... why do you look like you've seen a ghost?"

"I–it's nothing." She exits out of the app, shoving my phone back into my hand. Her entire demeanor has changed in a fraction of a second.

"What's going on, Noelle?"

"Okay, you can't be mad at me..."

The only thing that comes to mind with Winter is, "Did you fuck him?"

"No. Hell no."

"Then why are you nervous?"

"I–we–he kissed me. We kissed each other."

"Kissed?" I raise my brows, trying to keep the jealousy out of my tone. "Why? When? And how?"

"Because we were trying to make my ex jealous when I saw him at Fireside. His idea by the way. This was right before I left on vacation. And... how? I mean... how do two people kiss?"

"Did you enjoy it? Did he touch you?"

"I mean... he's not a bad kisser," She says honestly. Her eyes widen as she looks at me. "That doesn't mean I enjoyed it." She looks off to the side, biting her lip. "Okay, I enjoyed it like the tiniest bit." She lets out an exasperated sigh, digging herself deeper. "I just–Snow it was before I met you. I didn't know. And it felt like absolutely nothing. Just a kiss to make my ex jealous."

"Did he touch you?" I ask, wondering if I should break Winter's fingers or not.

"No. It was just a kiss with a little tongue…"

"Tongue?!"

She cringes, putting her hands on the side of my face. "It was just a kiss. A meaningless, worthless kiss. Nothing more. I forgot all about it until I saw his picture."

I really don't have a right to be mad or jealous because we weren't together. Shit, we're not even together now. "You kissed my… brother?"

"Hardly even a kiss…" She looks off to the side, running her hand down her throat. "Thing of the past." I'm silent as she fidgets under my gaze. "Are you mad? I mean, honestly you have no right to– "

Wrapping my hand around the back of her neck, I pull her toward, bringing her lips to mine. I tease the seam of her lips with my tongue, and she opens for me, letting our tongues meet. Slipping my hand underneath her sweater, I brush my fingertips over her nipple. She moans into my mouth, grabbing a fistful of my shirt. I pull away when I hear Jade approaching.

"Mad? No. Jealous? Yes. I also know Winter well enough to know he gave you much more than a little tongue."

She snorts with laughter, burying her face in my neck. "Nothing compares to kissing you."

"Thank you for telling me, because you really didn't have to."

"I'll always be honest."

"Yeah... I noticed you kept digging yourself deeper and deeper with your confession."

She grins. "It's that look you give. Felt like I was confessing a sin."

"Now I know the power of RBF."

She laughs as Jade reappears with fruit, a mimosa, and my coffee, setting it down on the table. "I'll be back with your blanket, Miss Frost."

"This looks amazing, Jade. Thank you." Noelle smiles and wastes no time digging in. "I'm feeling regal." She smiles, taking a bite of a chocolate covered strawberry and then a sip of her mimosa.

"I love how you appreciate the simple things."

"Not sure what's simple about a private jet..."

I chuckle. "True, but that's not what I meant. You find joy in... anything."

"If I'm not enjoying myself, what's the point?"

"I need to adopt that outlook."

"I think you're doing a pretty good job, Snow. We all get a little lost along the way."

I've never felt the peace that I've found in her. Losing my dad and then Kenna took a toll on me. I felt like I was carrying around this invisible boulder of grief that no one could see even though it was crushing me. After losing my dad, I didn't really have an opportunity to fall apart. I felt I had to keep it together for my mom, Winter, and North. Then with Kenna, the way I lost her, I don't know anyone who wouldn't lose a piece of themselves watching the person they love die.

Jade hands Noelle a blanket and picks up her now empty plate before disappearing again.

"Damn, you mowed that shit down," I say.

She climbs off my lap, yawning. "I was hungry, and now I'm sleepy. Take a nap with me?"

"I'll sleep anywhere with you." Finishing my coffee in a few gulps, I rise to my feet. "There's a bed this way."

"Of course there is." She follows behind me. When we get to the bed, she kicks off her moon boots and sprawls out on it. "This is so cozy."

I lie next to her, getting underneath the blanket. She immediately wraps herself around me, yawning. I can't help the smile that appears on my face.

"I'm happy you're here with me, Noelle."

"Where else would I be?"

Several hours later, we're back in Hope Valley. I'm holding Noelle's bags, waiting for her to unlock her apartment door. My nerves are getting the best of me. I didn't think I'd be nervous being at her place given we just spent the past five days together. This is different. This is *her* personal space.

Turning on the lights, she smiles at me. "It's not much, but it's home sweet home. I just re-decorated since…" Her voice trails off.

"It's perfect." I already know why she redecorated and don't care to dwell on the topic. "Did you want me to put these somewhere?"

"You're fine. I can take them to my room." She reaches for them, but I keep a hold on them.

"I can carry them."

"Alright." She turns, heading down the hallway, and I follow her. "In here."

I set them down on the bench at the foot of her neatly made bed. "I'm not seeing the organized chaos."

She smiles, looking around her room. "I never said I was like that all the time. Who has time for organization on vacation?"

"Touché. You have a very nice space. Thank you for inviting me."

Opening her suitcase, she pulls out what looks like a makeup bag. "I'm going to shower and change. Do you mind waiting?"

"Take your time."

"Make yourself at home." She smiles before disappearing into the bathroom.

Instead of sitting on her bed, I head back out to the living room. Her apartment is as warm and inviting as she is, decorated in earth tones. Various lush, green plants are scattered through the living room and kitchen. There are two large bookcases, filled with books, and the walls have art with a few pictures. Taking a closer look, she has quite a few with a woman who resembles her. It must be her sister. I can feel the love in the pictures.

Making myself at home, I sit on the couch. This past week has been a whirlwind. It's interesting how we go through life without someone until we meet, and then life is unimaginable without them. My phone vibrates with a text.

Winter: Are you back yet?
North: Where are we eating tonight?

We usually have a dinner after I get back from my vacation. The tradition started the first year after Kenna died and I went away. They claimed they missed me, which I'm sure they did, but I know the true reason was they didn't want me to be alone.

Snow: I'm eating at my place. You two can eat wherever you want.
Winter: Trading us in for Miss Mistletoe Mountain?
North: The woman from the picture?
Snow: Yeah. I'm at her place now.
North: Her place?
Winter: Not even an invite to meet her? Does she have a sister? We can make this a family affair.
Snow: You've already met her, Winter.
Winter: Have I?

That's how much Winter messes around. He doesn't even remember kissing her.

North: What about me?
Snow: She said she met you at Fireside at the bar and you kissed her to make her ex jealous.
North: Kissed???

I see Winter start typing and then stop a few times. A smile tugs at my lips imagining how much he's sweating right now out of fear of my response.

Winter: That's Miss Mistletoe Mountain??? Shit. Good thing I didn't take her home.
North: You gonna let that slide, Snow?

Snow: Chill. She wasn't interested in you.
Winter: Damn. She did tell me I need new pick up lines.
North: You realize they like you for your looks and not your
conversation, right?

I laugh, finding comfort in this piece of information.

Snow: Damn. She really wasn't interested in you. How does that
make you feel?
Winter: Honestly, a little hurt. I thought at least I could've taken
her home.
North: Now I really want to meet her if she's unphased by Winter.
Snow: You can be a third wheel if you want.
Winter: And fuck you, North. I am an amazing conversationalist.
North: Used all your brain power for that word huh?

Noelle appears, wrapped in a towel. "Let me put on some clothes."
She disappears into a small room off of the kitchen, reappearing with a
basket of folded clothes.

"All I'm seeing is you in a towel."

She laughs. "A voyeur after all."

Looking at my phone, Winter and North are going at each other in the
chat. I let out an exasperated sigh. They'll never grow up.

Snow: We'll get together sometime soon. Just not tonight. Okay?
I actually like her a lot. It's been a long time since I've wanted
someone in my space.
Winter: Damn. Miss Mistletoe Mountain has you in a hold.

Snow: Her name is Noelle.

Winter: I like my nickname better.

North: Tell Noelle I look forward to meeting her. Winter, you're a jackass.

Winter: Fuck you. Since Snow is abandoning us, want to meet up?

North: You're in my fucking living room dipshit.

Winter: Shit. Right. The edible kicked in. Have a good night, Snow. Can't wait to be an uncle.

North: I'll be the favorite.

Laughing, I shake my head at their exchange. It's been like this since we were kids. They annoy the hell out of me, but I wouldn't be here without them.

"Ready." Noelle appears in a short, black pleated skirt, giving me the perfect view of her legs, an oversized sweater, sneakers, and the necklace I gave her gleaming around her neck. "I can read your filthy thoughts from here. Feed me first. Then you can have me."

Tearing my eyes away from her legs, I give her a smile. "Alright." I stand, adjusting myself.

She shakes her head with a smirk on her lips and heads for the front door. I smack her ass, grabbing a handful, as she walks in front of me.

"Snow!" she yelps.

"What?" I pull her flush against me, wrapping my arm around her waist. "You wanted to torture me, Snowflake? Dressing up like this and not letting me unwrap you?"

"You know the stipulations." She looks up at me. "Feed me. Then fuck me."

I kiss her temple. "I'm so happy they fucked up our cabin reservations." I open the car door for her.

"Me too." She smiles before sliding into the front seat.

Getting in the driver side, I see she hasn't fastened her seatbelt. She's typing out a text on her phone. "Can you put your seatbelt on, please?" I fasten my own, hoping she doesn't think I'm being bossy. But I'm not sure I could survive a repeat of Kenna.

"Shit, Snow." She drops her phone, grabbing for the seatbelt. " I'm sorry. I was sending a text to my sister."

Once it's fastened, I start the car. "You don't have to apologize. I just... wouldn't want anything to happen to you. Even if you weren't with me."

"I always wear my seatbelt." She grabs my hand. "And Aspen tells me I drive like a grandma so..." I laugh heartily. "I've been driving since I was sixteen, but I still get nervous on the freeway. And we won't talk about weather conditions."

"I remember you being willing to walk the two and a half miles to the reindeer farm."

"Again," she sighs, stretching out her legs, causing her skirt to ride up. "I have you now. It doesn't need to be discussed."

14
Noelle

I was expecting Snow to have a large mansion. His home is still big, but cozy. It's modern with a touch of gothic. Strong, rich colors remind me of his personality. I couldn't contain my squeal when he showed me the library with floor to ceiling shelves. There's no other feeling like falling into a good book with a cozy blanket wrapped around you. After a delicious dinner, I couldn't wait to get back to the library.

He leans against the doorframe, watching me run my hand along the books. "You like books?"

"Love. What is the most well worn book on your shelves?"

"Books." He pushes away from the doorframe, walking behind the desk, and pulls a set down from the top shelf. They are in tatters. "Lord of the Rings. My grandpa got the trilogy to read, and when my dad was old enough to care– " I laugh " –he read them and they quickly became his favorites. Most kids had fairytales read to them, we did too by our mom, but my dad read us Lord of the Rings as a bedtime story."

"That's a beautiful memory. These books are definitely loved." I take them from his hands, carefully opening them. "They're... signed?" I gasp, staring at the signature.

"Yeah." He pulls a picture from the shelf, showing it to me. It's a tall gentleman, who looks similar to Snow, standing holding the same stack of books, although in the picture they're much less worn. "That's my dad. When I tell you he loved them, that man loved them. He found this set at an auction."

"This is insane." I mutter staring at the signature. "I shouldn't be holding these." I close the book, handing it back to him.

"I'll never sell. My dad taught me books were meant to be loved. What do you like to read?" He places them back on the shelf.

"Romance, fantasy, sci-fi. Honestly... I'll read anything as long as it has a dash of romance in it."

"A dash?" He chuckles.

"Yeah. There's something about love that sucks me in like a moth to a flame." I plop down on the couch.

He sits beside me, pulling my feet into his lap. "Are you a hopeless romantic?"

"Yes. I'll always believe in love. No love wasted. No love lost."

His brows knit together. "What does that mean?"

"Meaning, if I'm loving, I'm living. Love never goes to waste, and it isn't lost when we lose someone we love. What matters is that we love."

He holds my gaze, tilting his head to the side, and nods. "Never thought of it that way. No love wasted. No love lost. I like that." I smile, getting comfortable on the couch. "Did you want me to take you home?"

"No," I say a little too quickly.

He chuckles, taking off my shoes. "You're mine to keep tonight?"

"Yes." My breath hitches as he trails his fingertips up my leg.

Grabbing my ankle, he pulls until my back is flat on the couch. My skirt rides up, exposing my panties. He presses his body to mine as our lips meet. The weight of him on top of me feels like heaven. Slipping his hand under my sweatshirt, he pulls it off, and then unfastens my bra. I gasp as he rolls my nipple between his fingertips. Sitting up, he pulls me with him, setting me atop the desk.

"Your outfit is fitting." He tugs at my plaid skirt.

"Is that why you showed me your library? To seduce me?"

He kisses my navel, pulling my panties off. "I don't have to seduce you when you're already wet for me." I see him grab something out of the corner of my eye. Sitting up, he has a feathered pen in his hand. "Before I take you, I want a puddle underneath you."

"From a feather?" I giggle.

"I'm going to enjoy teaching you all the ways you can cum for me, Snowflake." He grabs the scarf that was hanging off the arm of the chair. "Close your eyes."

I follow his orders and he ties the soft scarf over my eyes. It smells like him. This alone heightens my anticipation. I'm wondering how he's going to make me cum with a feather... until he lightly brushes it over my nipple. I'm surprised by the current of pleasure it sends through my body. I feel my skin pepper with goosebumps. He drags the feather across my other nipple, giving me another jolt of pleasure, pulling the feather over the sensitive areas of my body.

Nipples, stomach, inner thighs... and then he barely teases the mound of my pussy. I'm not sure how long he does this for because I'm lost in the waves of bliss. My body becomes hypersensitive with each swipe and drag of the feather. I moan as he teases my nipples. My skin heats, and it feels near impossible to catch my breath as my climax builds.

"This feels so fucking good..." I breathe.

"You're dripping, but I want more."

He brushes the feather across my nipples– *back and forth, back and forth* –teasing me until, "Fuck, Snow. I'm so close..." I drag my nails across the desk, looking for anything to hold onto.

"Let go, Noelle," he whispers near my ear, still teasing my nipples.

And I do. Free falling straight into sweet oblivion. Stars light up in the darkness of my closed eyes. The climax pulls me under. Wave after wave. My voice becomes hoarse as my impassioned moans fill the room. He slows the teasing of my nipples, bringing me through the waves of my orgasm. My body twitches with pleasure when I hear him set the pen aside.

"You doubted me, Snowflake?" I hear the smile in his voice and feel his hands untying the scarf.

"I'll admit, I thought it was your hidden arrogance shining through," I say breathlessly.

A chuckle resonates in his chest as he pulls the scarf from my eyes. "It's not arrogance. It's confidence. Just how I'm confident I'm about to draw every last drop from you tonight."

He hoists me up, wrapping my legs around his waist and bringing my lips to his. My sensitive nipples brush against his chest, and I let out a needy moan as we kiss. I'm not sure where he's taking me until I feel the softness of a bed against my back. Opening my eyes, I look around to see we're in his room. It's dimly lit, but all I care to see is him. He unbuttons his pants, letting them fall to the floor and then climbs on top of me.

Kissing my neck, he asks, "Now can I have you?"

"I'm all yours."

He pushes into my wetness slowly, bringing my legs over his shoulders. I grip his forearms as he stretches me out, letting my legs fall open until they're hooked over his arms. He grips my hips, thrusting slow and deep. I match his rhythm, moving our hips in tandem.

"Snow..." I chant his name, on the cusp of another orgasm.

Reaching between us, he massages my clit. I inhale sharply, savoring the feel of him filling me up and commanding my senses.

"Come undone for me." He keeps the pressure on my clit.

"Fuck, keep it right there," I pant. "Right fucking– "

I shatter for him again, calling out his name.

"Good fucking girl," he growls, spreading my thighs further apart, as he pounds into me.

His thrusts are deep and relentless, hitting the spot that suspends me in a state of ecstasy. Grabbing my arms, he pins them above my head, keeping my wrists in his hold. His other hand wraps firmly around my throat, applying the right amount of pressure.

"Keep those legs open for me," he says, leaning forward, pressing his lips to mine. I moan into his mouth as I keep my legs up and open. "That's my girl, take every fucking inch."

"Your... girl..."

He lets out a mix of a moan and a growl, plunging into the depths of me. His body tenses as he teeters on the edge of his climax, falling into me seconds later. I move my hips with his, riding each current of pleasure. His body quakes with each wind of my hips.

"Ahhh..." He exhales as his dick twitches inside me. "You're ecstasy in human form."

He rolls to the side, pulling me with him. I get comfortable on his chest, listening to his racing heartbeat slow. "Snow..."

"Yeah?" He traces small circles on my back.

"I think I'm falling for you," I confess, holding my breath.

"You're catching up to me then." He kisses the top of my head.

Waking, I smile when I feel Snow's arm wrapped around me and his warm body pressed against my back. Our conversation replays in my head. He's falling for me too? Or has already fallen for me. Is it too soon to be falling for someone else? I'm not sure it matters with the way he makes me feel. It's as if we were meant to meet. Kismet. My mind is telling me I'm being ridiculous, but my heart feels at peace when I'm with him.

I'd stay wrapped up in his arms if I didn't have to pee. I try to wriggle out of his hold, but he's not budging.

"Snow..." I lightly tap his arm.

"Hmm..." he grunts.

"Unhand me so I can pee." Chuckling, he rolls over. "Thank you."

As I'm standing, he smacks my ass. "Nice view to wake up to." His voice is deep and gravelly. I watch his muscles flex as he stretches, admiring his morning salute tenting the sheets.

"You've been waking up with me the past five days... well, six now."

"Yeah, but now you're home with me. It's different."

I smile before turning toward the bathroom. It's about the size of my living room, if not bigger. Looking around, I notice his and hers sinks. His has all his stuff, but my brow furrows when I notice the hers side is cluttered with stuff too.

"What the hell?" I mutter, grabbing toilet paper.

Maybe he has a regular hookup? I wash my hands, side eyeing the skin care, annoyed she has good taste. Grabbing the mouth wash from his side, I rinse before returning to the bedroom. Snow is watching the news on the TV mounted to the wall.

"Can I borrow a shirt?"

"Yeah. They're in the closet," he says distractedly, typing out a text.

Unsurprisingly, it's expertly organized. Suits, pants, shirts, shoes, casual attire with splashes of color that make me smile. It fades when my eyes land on the women's clothing toward the back of the closet. From the boot lying haphazardly near a bench, he shares this space. I immediately exit, grabbing my skirt off the floor.

"Where's the library?" I avoid his gaze, pulling up the zipper.

He sits up. "You're leaving?"

"Yes." I answer plainly. "I need my clothes."

"Why?"

"I need my clothes, Snow." Tears sting my eyes. Of course this was all too good to be true. How dare he admit to falling for me when he's clearly sharing his life with someone else.

"Noelle – "

"Clothes," I demand.

"I'll get them." He rises from the bed.

As soon as he's gone, I squeeze my eyes shut, willing the tears to stay put. My heart is bruised from the recklessness it's been subjected to. He reappears, and I wipe my eyes before turning to face him. I grab my clothes from him, pulling on my sweatshirt. Now that I'm covered, I feel less vulnerable.

"What did I do?" he asks.

"Whose stuff is that, Snow?" I point toward the bathroom and closet, hobbling on one foot as I pull on my sneaker. He looks as though I struck him. His eyes widen. "Whose shit is that?" I ask through gritted teeth.

"It's not what you think..."

"Then what the fuck is it?"

"It's Kenna's stuff," he says softly.

His admission hurts more than if he were to tell me he was seeing someone else. My heart breaks for him and... me.

"Oh..." I scan the room, noticing the pictures of them.

I'm not sure what to say. I've never lost someone to know what he's going through, but the thought creeps in that maybe I'll never quite be enough for him. A second option. A filler for what could've been.

"Snow..." I break the silence, wiping away a stray tear.

"Noelle, I know how this looks, but it's not–it's been here for so long I don't even notice it."

I see a swirl of emotions in his eyes as tears pool in my own. "You owe me nothing, but I owe it to myself to not be somebody's second best option. M-Maybe you need more time or someone who isn't me. I know you loved her– " I look at the happy pictures of them " –love her, and I can't help but wonder is there any room left for me?"

"There is, Noelle." He takes a step toward me, grabbing my hands. "I know this is fucked up. I know it–it was so hard to do anything after she died. I couldn't bear the thought of getting rid of her stuff, so I left it as she did. Meeting someone else, let alone caring about someone else, wasn't a thought in my mind... then you happened."

"Snow..." I look away from him. "I'm in a tomb with remnants of you and her. Maybe I'm fucking selfish because... I don't want to be stuck in the past with you nor do I want to be in the present as your second best option."

"You're not– "

"I need space." I pull my hands from his. "This is a lot for me to take in, and I need to process."

"Noelle..." He gives me a pained expression. "Okay..." He nods his head, running his hands down his face. "Okay, I can respect that. Can I drive you back to your place at least, please?"

I nibble on my lip. "Sure."

He visibly relaxes. "Let me put some clothes on."

I nod, pulling the sleeves of my sweater over my hands, and hug myself. He quickly moves around the room, putting on clothes. A few minutes later, he straightens up after tying his sneaker, and holds out his hand to me. I look at it, hesitating, before placing my palm in his and following him through the house. He opens a door to a garage that has multiple cars parked in it and leads me to a white car, opening the door for me. I slide into the white leather seat and fasten my seatbelt, resting my head against the window. The scent of him invades my senses when he gets in beside me.

I'm not sure what to say, so I keep my eyes glued to the side mirror as he takes me back to my place. I feel like a bitch for making a big deal about his late fiancée's stuff. Hearing about his fiancée and seeing her stuff, the space they shared, is a lot for me. I don't want to be frozen in time with constant reminders of the life he didn't get.

A ripple of panic grips me when he turns onto the street my apartment complex is on. What if we never see each other again? What if this is it? I steal a glance at him, hoping this isn't the end. I just need some time. We've spent the past week together. Space will do both of us some good... hopefully.

He parks, cutting the engine, and gets out of the car. Seconds later, he opens my door, holding his hand out to me. I take it, getting out and standing in front of him. He cups my chin, making me look up at him.

"I'm going to try like hell to give you space. If you're doubting the connection we have or my feelings, know that all I've seen and wanted since I met you is... you."

He gives me a kiss that steals my breath and makes me question what the fuck I'm doing asking for space. But that's the problem, I don't know if I'm just swept up in the gravity of him, losing sight of myself.

Later in the week, I lie with my head in Aspen's lap. She takes out my braids while I stuff a handful of fries into my mouth and tell her what happened with Snow.

"I really don't see what the problem is," she says, setting the braiding hair she just pulled loose aside.

I glare up at her. "How can you not see the problem?"

"I see *your* problem, but I'm looking at the bigger picture. Snow wined you, dined you, spoiled you, and fucked you in a span of five days when most men can't even fathom doing that in a lifetime. You're dumb if you think that man isn't all about you. No one does that purely to knock boots. He cares about you. So my question is, what are you afraid of?"

"You're supposed to be on my side," I say, shoving another handful of fries into my mouth.

"I am. When you're not being a stubborn brat. Again, what are you afraid of?"

Delaying my response, I shove another handful of fries into my mouth. She smacks the center of my forehead. "Ow!" I laugh, covering my face.

"I asked you a question. Answer it."

"I am! You don't have to abuse it out of me."

"I do when you're casting around for excuses in that dense skull of yours."

"My skull isn't dense!"

She lets out an exasperated sigh. "It is when you're threatened by his dead girlfriend. D-E-A-D! She gone, sis!"

"You're going to hell!" I cackle. "Be respectful!"

She covers her mouth. "You're right. Respectfully, she is no longer with us. Yet you are still threatened."

"I'm not threatened. I just don't... want another repeat of Malcolm. I don't want to be a second best option again."

She scoffs. "Can't believe you're letting that piece of shit steal your peace. His mother should've swallowed and spared us his existence."

I hold my stomach as I laugh. "You act like he hurt you!"

"Collateral damage. You're my sister. Malcolm isn't shit and never will be. And I'm going to be frank, it's not fair you're threatened by Snow's past when you're holding onto yours too."

15
SNOW

I CAN'T DENY NOELLE'S right. I'd have a similar response if I were to go to her house and see her ex's things lying around as if he still lived there. Understanding where she's coming from doesn't make this situation any easier.

"It's time to move on ..." I whisper out loud, lying on my bed as I stare at the ceiling.

Kenna and I bought this house a few months before I proposed. After she passed, I considered selling, but like her clothes, I couldn't bring myself to do it. Living without Kenna seemed unbearable until the days ticked on without her. Her stuff, this home–shit, even me–slowly became relics, fading seamlessly into the present while still being stuck in the past. Until Noelle jolted me awake, making me want to live. It's been almost five days without her and I feel like I'm going through withdrawals.

Grabbing for my phone, I contemplate texting her, but remind myself that I promised her space. Instead, I make a call to Brielle. It rings a few times before she picks up.

"I can't believe you're calling me." There's a smile in her voice. "How are you?"

"I'm alright."

"Are you sure? If you're calling me, something probably isn't," she teases.

I let out a sigh, pinching the bridge of my nose. "I need help."

"With what?"

The unexpected emotions plummet me. "With Kenna's stuff." My voice cracks. "It's time for me to let go." Admitting it to Brielle makes what I'm about to do a reality.

"Yeah, of course." I hear her moving around. "I'll be there in fifteen minutes."

"Thank you, Brielle."

"I'll be right there."

Hanging up the phone, I pull myself out of bed to take a shower and make myself look decent after lying around the past couple of days. Thankfully, I don't have to be back in the office until the New Year.

My phone rings as I'm pulling on a pair of jeans after my shower. Winter's name flashes across my screen.

"What's up, bro?"

"Nothing. You fell off the face of the earth. We wanted to check on you." North joins the call seconds later.

"Did you drown in Noelle or what?" North asks.

I put my phone down, pulling on my t-shirt. "Something like that."

"You're being elusive," Winter says suspiciously. "Do you need us to come over?"

"Nah. Not today. I have some stuff to take care of."

"Either tell us what's going on or we'll be barging through your front door," North threatens.

"How are the two of you so fucking dramatic?" I sigh exasperatedly. "Brielle's coming over to help me go through Kenna's stuff."

"Shit..." Winter mutters.

"Are you sure you don't want us there?" North asks.

"Positive, but I appreciate both of you."

"I thought you were blowing us off for Miss Mistletoe Mountain, and I just want her to know we were here first," Winter says.

I chuckle. "Really? Jealous are you?"

"Winter loves all the attention. You know this." North says.

"Mom and Dad forced me to share the spotlight with you two. Miss Mistletoe Mountain will have to earn a spot."

"Well... I'm not sure – " Before I can finish my sentence, the doorbell rings. "I've gotta go. That's Brielle."

"Tell Brielle we said hello," North says.

"Let us know if you need anything, bro, and we'll be there."

We say our goodbyes, and hanging up, I open the door.

Brielle holds a coffee out to me. "Hope you still like your coffee the same. If not, oh well."

I take it from her hand as she steps into the foyer. "Thank you." I chuckle. "And I do."

She looks around, turning on the spot. "Glad to see you at least tried to give it your personality with the darker colors, but it clashes with Kenna's décor. We'll get to that another day. Show me her stuff so we can get started."

I lead the way to the bedroom, opening the door to the closet. "I wasn't sure if you'd want some of her stuff or even what to do with it..."

She sets her coffee down, shrugging out of her jacket, and rolling up her sleeves. "There are some boxes in the back of my car. Go get them, please." I take the keys dangling from her hand.

When I return, I'm amazed how fast she's going through everything. There are bags, clothes, shoes, and jackets strewn across the closet floor.

She points to a pile. "That stuff is for donation. I'll take it to the women's shelter. This pile is for Isla." Isla is Kenna's little sister.

"Okay." I assemble the boxes, writing the names of where they're going on the sides.

Brielle continues sorting through Kenna's stuff while I pack it into boxes. The side that belonged to her is nearly empty.

She holds up a dress with a smile on her face. "This fucking dress." I furrow my brows, looking at it, trying to recall where it's from. "She wore it the night – "

"She met me." I finish the sentence for her, remembering Kenna in the pastel blue dress.

"I practically had to drag her ass out of the house for that party, and I never let her forget it. And here– " she points at a spot on the dress " –is where she spilled her wine when she bumped into you."

"I remember that, and she tried to blame me." I smile at the memory.

Brielle tosses her head back with laughter. "She couldn't walk in heels to save her life. It all worked out though because she met you."

"Yeah…" I watch her set it in the plastic bag for the trash. She catches my gaze, moving it out of my way. "So, what triggered you to want to let go of her stuff?"

"Um…" I sit on the floor beside her. "The trigger was Noelle."

"She came home with you?" She smiles.

"Yeah, we were inseparable our entire vacation."

"What happened?"

I look down at my hands. "She came over the evening we got home and spent the night. When she woke in the morning she saw all of Kenna's stuff scattered around as if she were still alive. A little fucking morbid..."

"And she left?"

"She said she needed space because it's a lot to process." I fill Brielle in on the conversation I had with Noelle a few days ago.

"Can you blame her?" she asks. "I mean look at all this shit, Snow. It had to feel like a slap in the face for her."

"I know, I know... I fucking know." Enunciating each word as I bang my head against the dresser behind me. "It honestly faded into the background to the point it didn't cross my mind."

"You're doing this for you, right? Not for Noelle. No matter how much you like her."

"I think I love her..." I admit. "I'm a fucking mess. I shouldn't be talking about this while cleaning out Kenna's stuff."

"News flash, Snow. She's dead. These clothes aren't going to haunt you anymore than you've already haunted yourself."

I laugh indulgently. "Thank you for never tiptoeing around me."

"Fuck your feelings." She grins. "Honestly, Kenna would want you to be happy. Even if it is without her."

"You're right." I sigh, rubbing my eyes. "I'm cleaning out Kenna's stuff because I need to move on for my own sake. Earlier this week, I had a therapy session with Dr. Yearwood. He helped me find the reassurance I needed to finally do this."

Brielle smiles, touching my hand. "I'm proud of you. You've come a long fucking way. You deserve to be happy."

"Thanks, Brielle." I squeeze her hand back.

"Always here any time you need a reality check."

I chuckle. "That's honestly why I've avoided you. I knew you wouldn't let me live in my memories."

"Oh, I know." She laughs, shaking her head. "But I also knew you weren't ready. You've come around in your time. That's what matters."

"Took me five years…"

"So fucking what?" She shrugs. "You're here, aren't you? Celebrate that."

It seems mundane, and a little ridiculous, to celebrate my existence. The past five years have been anything but mundane and ridiculous. They were brutal, but here I am. Still standing. I take out my phone, sending a text to Winter and North.

Snow: Want to go out for drinks tonight?
Winter: You want to go out? As in leave the house for drinks?
North: Is this Snow?
Snow: Yes you dumb fucks. Do you want to go out or not? Before I change my mind.
Winter: Of course I want to go out.
Snow: For a few drinks. Not to get fucking hammered.
North: We can go somewhere that isn't as busy as Fireside if you want. Ease you back into society.

"And that's it." Brielle stands, looking around at the now half empty closet.

"Damn." I take it in. "Haven't seen that side empty in a long fucking time."

"How do you feel?" She rests her hand on my arm.

"I feel… relieved. Thank you for doing this for me."

"Don't mention it. Is there anything else of hers here?"

"Uh... yeah. Her stuff is still in the bathroom and then... the pictures. What the fuck do I do with the pictures?"

"Do you want to keep them?"

I take a deep, cleansing breath. "Honestly, no. While the captured memories are happy, it just makes me remember what happened. It's time to let them go."

"I got you." She turns without another word, and heads toward the bathroom.

"I'll be out back." I holler, not wanting to know what she does with the pictures.

Once I'm outside, I pull out my phone.

Snow: We can go to Fireside.
North: Bet. What time?
Snow: They have food there, right?
Winter: Some of the best in the valley.
Snow: 6?
North: See you there.

Sitting on a chair that's in the sun, I sprawl out. We get enough snow to enjoy it in Hope Valley, but today is one of those rare winter days that's unusually warm. Everything feels right about today. Even if I am missing Noelle. My fingers itch to send her a text. Opening my phone, the only thing in our message thread is the picture of us on the way home. After typing out a million monologues, I decide to keep it simple.

Snow: I'm better at showing my feelings than writing them.

Snow: I miss everything about you, Snowflake.

I stare at my phone, hoping she'll respond or at least feel how much I miss her. I'll give her space, but I can't promise her distance. Everything with us has happened fast. The physical quickly turned into emotional, and now I can't imagine her not being in my life. I know she feels it too. She doesn't have to tell me when I see it in the depths of her brown eyes and feel it with each touch.

I close my eyes, thinking about going out tonight when a thought comes to my mind. Opening my phone again, I pull up Wilder's number. He picks up after a few rings, letting out an exasperated sigh. I grin.

"If you're calling me to complain, you'll have to wait until we resume regular business hours."

"Nice to talk to you too, Wilder."

"What do you want on this lovely day, Snow?"

"I wanted to thank you for booking my Christmas vacation and also invite you to drinks with my brothers and me tonight." A long silence ensues. "Um... are you there?"

"Yeah. Yeah. I'm here. I'm just shocked you're inviting me to go out with you. Did you hit your head while on vacation?"

I chuckle. "No, well, technically, yes–but this invitation is about to expire if you keep talking shit."

"I'm shocked is all!" He laughs. "We've known each other ten years, and you haven't invited me anywhere besides a meeting."

"I know. I'm not sure if this sounds pathetic or not, but I consider you a friend, and wanted you to come out with me tonight."

"No. Not pathetic at all. I'll go. What time and where? I had to wait for the initial shock to wear off."

"Six at Fireside. Bring your girlfriend if you'd like."

"I will. We'll see you at six."

I end the call, smiling to myself. It will be nice to get to know Wilder outside of the office setting. I don't blame him for not knowing how to take my invitation. Brooding, stoic, RBF – all the terms Noelle uses – are perfect to describe me. I've had a wall around me the past five years that she tore down in five days, letting the light in.

A little while later, Brielle joins me by the pool, interrupting my thoughts. "I'm done." She exhales, sitting on a chair beside me. "Now what will you do?"

I check my phone again before responding, realizing I was sitting lost in thought. When I see Noelle hasn't read my texts, I reluctantly slide my phone back into my pocket.

"Sell it. I spoke with a realtor. They're waiting on my word to list."

"You're diving headfirst into change." She smiles.

Bringing my hands together, I rub my thumb against my palm. "I appreciate what I had with Kenna. When she crosses my mind, I want to remember good things. This house reminds me of nothing but shattered dreams. I went through the worst time of my life in those walls. Noelle was right... it's a tomb."

She pats my arm, giving me a sympathetic smile. "I'm happy to see you living again."

"Thanks..." I return her smile, looking at the house.

"Where are you going to stay in the meantime? You don't sound like you want to be here anymore."

"I'm going to ask North if I can stay with him while I look for a place. Winter is too wild for me."

"I know. I see him around quite a bit. Always asking if I'm tired of Ezra."

I laugh, shaking my head. "He's full of himself."

"Well," she stretches, sitting back in the seat. "We had a little thing after you and Kenna got together."

"What?" I give her a look of disbelief.

"It's true and honestly something that's hard to admit."

I try to pull up memories of Winter from that time. It was one of the only times since dad died that he wasn't flying off the handle. "That means you two were a thing for months."

"Correct." She nods her head, smiling.

"What happened?"

"He was clearly in love with someone else."

"Ah... yeah. Figured."

"Yep. So when he asks me if I'm tired of Ezra, I ask him if he's gone back to her yet."

"I know that shuts him up."

She grins. "Works like a charm every time."

"He'll get there... eventually. He's been doing good lately. Proud of how far he's come."

"You need to tell him that more often, Snow." Her eyes meet mine. "I know you two had your shit in the past and you're his little brother, but he looks up to you."

"Me?"

"Yeah, you." She points at me, giving me a look of exasperation. "When he's not trying to get in my pants," I laugh, "we talk when I work the bar at Fireside. He needs to hear that you're proud of him more often because he feels like a fuck up."

SNOW KING CATCHES HIS SNOWFLAKE

"I mean... he is." She punches my arm. "Fuck!" I rub it, cowering away from her. "But... we all fuck up. Doesn't mean I love him any less. Wait... do you care about Winter?"

"As a friend, yeah."

"Huh..." I lean back in the chair.

I may still harbor a little resentment toward him for not being there after dad died, leaving me to take care of mom and North. Then when he did come back, he brought nothing but trouble. Gambling debts, drugs, countless nights where I had to bail him out of jail, and it just kept piling on. Then Kenna died, and he still couldn't get his shit together for me. I thought we would always have each other's back and he didn't have mine when I needed him most. So yeah... a lot of fucking resentment.

"I better get going." Brielle stands. "Told Ezra I was on my way back. Don't want him to worry."

"Okay. By the way, we'll be at Fireside tonight. Me, Winter, and North."

"Really?" She smiles. "Finally coming out to see what we've built?"

"Yeah... thanks for never giving up on me."

"Thank yourself. I'll see you tonight."

Later that evening, I pull up to North's place. He meets me outside before I can even open my door. Stepping out of the car, he pulls me into a hug.

"Good to see you, brother."

"Yeah, you too." I clap him on the back. "Thanks for letting me crash at your place."

"Don't mention it. Where are your bags?"

"I can get them," I say, heading toward the back of the car.

"And I can help."

North is one of the kindest people I know. Only sees the good in people and wears his heart on his sleeve. Both are admirable characteristics, but it also leaves him vulnerable to get taken advantage of. The last girl he dated tried to take him for a ride. It hit him hard when he realized she wanted him for the money and didn't actually like him at all.

I follow him upstairs. "You can stay up here. That way you feel like you have your own space."

"You're my brother, North. We used to share a bedroom, remember?"

He smiles, reminding me of dad. "True, but I still want you to be comfortable."

"I'm always comfortable with you and Winter. Speaking of, where is he?"

"He's meeting us there. Said he had some business to take care of."

"That's what he's calling being a professional man whore now? Business? May as well call himself a gigolo."

He chuckles. "I'm sure he'd wear the title proudly."

"Do you think..." My voice trails off as I plop down on the bed. "Do you think I'm too hard on Winter?"

He crosses his arms, leaning against the doorframe, furrowing his brow with thought. "He definitely needs tough love... but," his eyes meet mine, "he needs the love of his brother more."

I nod, taking in his words. "I called him while I was on vacation. It was the first time in a while we had a real conversation. I missed that."

"He told me about it. Not the conversation, but that you called him. He was so fucking happy. Winter knows he fucked up. Reminding him constantly isn't doing him, or you, any favors."

"You're right..."

"You're letting go of the past. Afford Winter the same grace." He holds my gaze before pushing away from the doorframe. "I'm going to get ready."

He leaves me with my thoughts. Sometimes we need a perspective outside of our own to see a picture clearly.

Fireside is a unique experience. If a bar, club, and restaurant were to have a baby – that's how I'd describe it. The atmosphere is reminiscent of sitting beside a fire, enjoying time with friends. Cozy, yet brimming with energy. This the first place I've ever been that both the drinks and food are delicious.

Brielle approaches our table with a smile on her face. "Had to come see for myself that you're actually here." She gives me a hug.

"You and Ezra have built something truly amazing."

"I can't wait for you to see the brewery."

"No Ezra tonight?" Winter chimes in, raking his eyes over Brielle.

She smiles, leaning over the table, holding his gaze. "We can meet in the supply closet if you want? I know all you need is a minute."

I nearly choke on my drink as North howls with laughter. Winter stares at her with a smile on his face, tipping back his drink as he finishes it off.

"Always loved your feistiness."

My phone lights up with a text, catching my attention. Picking it up, my heart drums in my chest when I see who it's from.

Snow: I miss everything about you, Snowflake.

Noelle: Even the pepper spray?

Smiling at my phone I respond instantaneously. I don't give a fuck how desperate I look to talk to her.

Snow: No... not that. Unless it's the only way I can see you again.

"Who has you smiling at your phone like that?" Winter asks. "Miss Mistletoe Mountain?" I ignore Winter, waiting for her response. "Here comes Ezra. I'm going to tell him you were hitting on me, Brielle."

"Remember that glorious time when he gave you a black eye?"

I pull my eyes away from my phone. "You two fought?"

"In order for there to be a fight, the other person has to fight back. Ezra straight clocked him." North fills me in, trying to hold in his laughter, but fails miserably.

"When was– " Before I can finish my sentence, Ezra appears with two women.

"Babe," Ezra says to Brielle. "You need to mark the table as occupied when you seat someone at it."

I don't hear what's said next, I'm focused on the woman to the right of Ezra. "Noelle?"

Her eyes are on her phone, typing out a text. She doesn't look up until she's finished, and my phone vibrates the same time our eyes meet.

"Snow... I was just..." She points at her phone.

"This is the guy you've been in your feelings about?" The girl to the left of Ezra points at me. "Thank the fucking heavens you're here. Do you know what it's like having to listen to my sister – " Noelle's glare cuts her off. "Hi, I'm Aspen. Elle has told me sooooo, so, so much about you." She holds out her hand.

I shake it, keeping my eyes on Noelle. "Snow. Nice to meet you. These are my brothers, Winter and North." I point to them.

"Hi." Aspen shakes their hands.

"Nice to put a name to the lips." Winter extends his hand to Noelle.

"Don't get yourself fucked up tonight," I warn.

Noelle smiles, shaking his hand. "Uh... nice to meet you too."

Brielle pulls Noelle into a hug, startling her. "Good to see you again."

She looks at me out of the corner of her eye as she responds to Brielle. "You too. It was a pleasant surprise to see Ezra hosting."

"I was trying to give them the best table," Ezra says, smiling.

"They can sit with us," North offers, his eyes focused on Aspen. If Aspen is anything like Noelle, he's in for a ride.

Noelle shoves her hands into her back pockets. The light catches the charms on the necklace around her neck, making me smile. She didn't take it off. Her hair is different. The braids are gone, and it's in its curly, natural state. I'm convinced she always looks stunning. Aspen looks to Noelle, waiting for her to answer. When she doesn't, she nudges her.

"Yeah... we can sit here. If you don't mind?" She looks at me. "We're waiting on a friend. She'll be here soon."

As if I'd fucking mind. "Join us." I smile at her.

"No one cares about my opinion here?" Winter asks.

"No," Ezra answers. "Not a soul."

Winter and Ezra go back and forth with North mediating, but I could care less. Noelle is here, and everything fades to the background in her presence. She sits beside me, meeting my gaze once she's settled. It takes everything in me to not lean forward and kiss her.

"Did Brielle invite you?" I ask, pulling my eyes away from her lips.

"No. Was she supposed to?"

"No it's just... we've ended up in the same spot again by chance."

She gives me a brilliant smile. "Don't worry. I don't have any pepper spray tonight."

"Can't even pretend to be mad about that."

She laughs, and I soak it up. "I'm honestly surprised you're out. Sounded like you didn't get out much when we talked."

"I don't but wanted to celebrate."

"What are you celebrating?" She leans closer to me.

"Change." I grab my glass of whiskey, looking into it. "And still being here after not wanting to be for so long..."

"Snow..." I give her my attention. "Can we go somewhere and talk?" She glances at the terrace with fire pits blazing on them.

"Y-Yeah." I stumble over the word.

"Aspen, I'll be back," she says as she stands.

Aspen waves her off, laughing at something North said. I know him well enough to know he's not that funny. Winter is now in a pleasant conversation with Ezra and Brielle as if they weren't fighting moments ago.

"After you." I gesture toward the terrace and follow behind her.

16
Noelle

TAKING SPACE FROM SNOW with the way he occupies my thoughts was a joke. Aspen is sick of hearing me talk about him. I told her *everything*, three times over, and again on the way here tonight. I wanted him to come back as soon as he left. Being at his place, seeing all his late fiancée's stuff, was a lot for me to take in. Even though I wanted him to stay, I knew I needed time to process not only being at his place, but our time together too. I thought time apart would bring clarity. It only brought me loneliness. Our physical attraction is fire, but our emotional connection is electric.

Stopping in front of a firepit, I look up at him. "You'd think you're tattooed on my brain with the way I think about you."

He smiles, visibly relaxing. "I could say the same about you."

"I–I..." My voice trails off, trying to find my words. "I don't want you to settle for me, Snow. Or to be a second best option. It's not my place to feel uncomfortable about your late fiancée's things being in your house. You two shared a life together, and I respect you having to do things in your own time. But... I don't want you to be stuck in the past with her and miss the present with me."

He takes a step toward me, closing the gap between us, and grabs my hand. "I can admit I was stuck in the past. Then you happened." He interlaces his fingers with mine. "And each passing moment we shared, caused the past to feel distant. Remember that flicker of desire for more you talked about?" I meet his gaze, nodding my head. "It's turned into a flame, and you were the fuel."

Butterflies swarm in my stomach. All I can do is stare at him as if his words put a spell on me.

"Noelle." He wraps his arm around my waist, pulling me flush against him. I can feel his heart beating as wildly as mine. "I know you might doubt how I feel about you – "

"That's just it, I've spent the past few days trying to doubt you. But it's like trying to deny the existence of the other half of my soul."

His lips crash into mine, and I burn for him. Days felt like an eternity. Aspen says I'm dramatic. Maybe I am. But no one feels what I do when his words sink into my soul and his touch worships my existence. I wrap my arms around his neck, intertwining our tongues, and moaning in his mouth. If I could spend my days wrapped up in him, I would. He pulls away and I give him a dazed look.

"If I don't stop, I'm going to bend you over that railing."

"You make that sound like a bad thing." I smile.

He chuckles smoothly. "I honestly think you're the voyeur in this relationship."

"Relationship?" I pull back, getting a better view of his face.

"You are made for me, Noelle. And I'm made for you. We can take things slow, but I want–need–you to be mine."

"Is there anything slow about us?"

"No." He smiles.

Holding his gaze, I say, "I'll be yours." Standing on my tiptoes, I press my lips to his.

"Let's get back inside before Brielle and Ezra have our sex tape on their cameras."

I cackle as he wraps his arm around my neck, leading us back to the table. We clearly weren't missed. Aspen is enjoying conversation with Winter, Brielle, and Ezra. A tall man and a woman have joined the table in our absence. The man smiles at Snow.

"Thought you left early," he says, shaking Snow's hand.

"Nah, I was talking to my girlfriend." The man's jaw goes slack as he stares between me and Snow. I grin, loving he called me his girlfriend. "Wilder, this is Noelle. Noelle, this is Wilder."

I giggle, looking up at Snow. "He talked so much shit about you while we were on vacation."

"This doesn't surprise me in the slightest." Wilder smiles. "I'd be concerned if he didn't." He turns to the woman beside him. "This is my girlfriend, Luna."

"Nice to meet you both." She shakes our hands. "Wilder may give you a hard time, but he admires you."

"Luna, please don't give away all my secrets," Wilder jokes.

"Admire?" Snow smiles.

"Did you know he has an ego?" I point at Snow.

"Hell yeah." Wilder chuckles. "One of the worst."

Looking up, I see Eve heading our way. She's been out of town for work and missed my "dramatics".

When she reaches us, she pulls me into a hug. "You're looking radiant."

"Snow, this is – "

"Eve." Snow finishes my sentence. "I–" he steals a glance at Winter who looks on the verge of puking " –how are you?"

"You two know each other?" I ask, raising a brow.

"Yes, she dated – "

"Winter." Eve's tone is venomous, as she whips around, locking eyes with him.

Realization sets in. Winter is the man who broke her heart. "Shit."

"Yeah..." Snow says as we watch their exchange.

"E-Eve." The confidence he wore when I met him is gone.

"That's all you have to fucking say, my name, after breaking off our engagement?"

"You're the woman he's in love with," Brielle says, pointing at her.

"Love?" Eve's eyes cut to Brielle. "Winter King isn't capable of love." She rounds on me, glaring. "And you're dating his brother?"

"Put your claws back in, Eve, before I have to pull them out," Aspen warns. "It's not Noelle's fault you got your heart broken."

Eve's eyes soften as she looks at me. "I'm sorry. I shouldn't have – I'm happy for you. I am."

"I can leave," Winter says, attempting to get up.

Eve leans across the table, catching his wrist before he can move. "No. Stay. I'd love to catch up." Her crazed look says otherwise.

"Um... give me a minute." I gently pull on Eve's arm. She doesn't budge until Aspen grabs her other one. She glares at Winter as we pull her away from the table. Moving out of view, I step in front of her.

"I know he hurt you, Eve."

"You don't know." Her eyes well with tears. "You have no fucking idea," she whispers.

The pain in her eyes hurts me. I hug her as she cries. Aspen wraps her arms around us.

"I wish I could invoke that kind of fear in a man," Aspen says longingly.

Eve and I laugh. "What?" Eve asks.

"Did you see his face?" Aspen asks. "It's as though he saw his reckoning and life flash before his eyes at the same time."

"He did look terrified." I rub Eve's back. "How have you two avoided each other all these years?"

Eve sniffles, and I grab a napkin off a nearby table, handing it to her. "*He* avoided me. I've practiced full monologues of what I would say to him when we crossed paths. And all I wanted to do in that second was throat chop him."

Aspen and I try to swallow our laughter. "I think your presence is a throat chop to him."

Eve squeezes her eyes shut. "I'm sorry for being a bitch. I was just – "

"Caught up in the moment?" I offer her a sympathetic smile.

"Yeah..." She looks away from me. "I think I'm going to go. I don't want to ruin your night."

"Please, if anything you're adding spice," Aspen says, wiggling her fingers as if she's sprinkling spices.

"We'd love for you to stay but understand if you'd rather leave."

She nibbles on her lip, glancing at the table. "I don't know... I guess a drink wouldn't hurt at this point. If you're with Snow, I'll have to be around Winter again at some point."

"You're not disowning me?" I tease.

"Hell no." She tears her eyes away from the table. "Snow is one of the good guys. You deserve that, Elle. Especially after dealing with a piece of shit like Malcolm."

"Who?" I knit my brows together.

"Look at the magic of good dick." Aspen smiles at me with pride. "She doesn't even remember his name."

We share a laugh before Eve composes herself to return to the table. She doesn't acknowledge Winter even though he can't take his eyes off her. Everyone stares between them for a moment, waiting for a bomb to detonate.

"Are we going to order drinks or just stare at each other?" Eve asks with a smile.

"First round is on the house," Ezra announces.

"You guys don't have to do that." Snow drapes his arm over my shoulders as I sit next to him.

"Of course we don't." Brielle smiles. "But we want to."

The tension that kicked off our evening dissipates when the drinks start flowing. It turns into an amazing night of food, karaoke (none of us can carry a tune to save our lives), dancing, and laughing until our stomachs hurt.

I lean into Snow as I slow dance with him at the end of the night. "Tired?" His hand rests on the small of my back while the other holds my hand with my palm pressed against his chest.

"No." I smile. "Happy."

He kisses my forehead. "It's so good to see your smile."

"Are you ready to get out of here?" I look up at him.

"Yeah, I came with North. Did you bring your car?"

"I did. Do you want to come back to my place? It's not that I don't want to go to your place, it's just that mine is closer and I'm trying to desperately jump your bones."

He flashes me a smile. "No need to explain what's already understood."

"Do you think North could give Aspen a ride back to her place?"

He glances at them. They've been talking all night. "Does it look like he'd mind?"

"No. Let me go tell her we're leaving." We make our way over to them, saying goodbye to Brielle and Ezra too.

"Bye, sis." Aspen hugs me. "Enjoy getting dicked down."

I groan, covering my face. "I wish I could say it's the alcohol, but this is how she is all the time."

"Hey, you didn't have to listen to yourself carry on about him every waking moment for days. May as well moan about it... literally." She smirks.

"Bye, Aspen." I push Snow in the opposite direction. "Nice to meet you North. She's your problem tonight." I stop in my tracks, turning back to Aspen. "Where's Eve?"

"She left. Said she had an early meeting tomorrow."

My brows knit together. Why wouldn't she had said goodbye? "Okay. I'll text her."

Pulling my phone out of my purse, I send her a text.

Noelle: Left without saying goodbye?

She replies within seconds.

Eve: You were having a moment with Snow. I'm a lot of things. But I'm no cock blocker.
Noelle: You've always been a cock enthusiast. You're okay, right?
Eve: I had fun. Want to go to dinner tomorrow? Just me, you, and Aspen?

Noelle: I'd love that. Love you.
Eve: Have fun getting your guts rearranged.

I gasp, glancing up at Snow who has a smile on his face as he reads her last text. "As you can see, they really advocate for my sexual well-being."

"I'm reaping the benefits." Snow smiles, grabbing my hand as we walk out to my car.

There's no place I'd rather be than lost in heated passion with Snow, taking me to heights only we know. Coming up for air after diving between my thighs, he gives me a debonair smile. I watch, attempting to catch my breath, as he unbuttons his jeans. My center aches with wanton desire to feel him inside me as if my essence isn't already coating his lips.

Who was I to deny myself such pleasures?

Naked, he hovers over me, kissing every inch of my body. I take a sharp inhale of breath as he swirls his tongue around my nipple. Wrapping my legs around his waist, my eyes roll back as he rolls his hips, pressing his length against my center. Reaching down between us, I wrap my hand around him.

"Always ready…" he mutters against my lips. Sitting up, he grabs my leg, coaxing me to roll onto my stomach. Gripping my hips, he pulls my ass back into his lap.

"Look up, Snowflake." I feel his hand sliding up my throat, coming to a stop underneath my chin. Our gazes meet in the mirror on the closet door.

"I want you to watch as I fuck any remaining doubt out of you." He lines himself up with my entrance, his brown eyes holding mine. "Because you, Snowflake, are my present and future." My breath hitches as he pushes into my wetness. Leaning forward, he tightens his hold on my throat. "I need you to understand that." He whispers in my ear before grazing his teeth against my neck.

Goosebumps pepper my skin as he sinks into me. Maybe I'm a voyeur after all because the sight of us, moving together in rhythm, has me in a trance. I watch his hand that's around my throat slide over my breasts, teasing them, before disappearing between my thighs, massaging my pearl.

Grabbing a fistful of my curls with his other hand, he thrusts into me slow and deep. "Look at you taking all of me. You're all I think of." He keeps his eyes locked with mine in the mirror. "All I see. We're made for each other."

His smooth, deep voice, each stroke and circle of his fingertips entices me closer to the edge. I indulge in the feel of him claiming me, leaving no room for apprehension between us. When it comes to matters of the heart, I was making logical, safe choices. I've been craving shared laughter, a kiss on the forehead, being vulnerable, and a touch that reaches beyond my skin and caresses my soul. I've found that with Snow. A level of intimacy only we know.

Sweat makes our skin slick as we move together. Releasing my hair, he slides it down my body, and grips my hip. His pace quickens, and I feel myself edging release. Fisting the sheets, I arch my back, burying my face as an orgasm rips through me.

"Good girl." He smacks my ass, soothing it seconds later as he rubs it before squeezing it. "Give me those waves." I can barely hear his praise as

I surrender to the pleasure. To him. "Keep that ass up for me." He grips my hips, and I arch my back, listening to his command.

Another cord of tension wraps itself around me, tightening with each thrust, until it snaps and I open for him again. My body quakes with sheer ecstasy as he finds his own bliss seconds after me. I slide up and down his shaft, getting everything he's got, before dissolving onto the mattress. Rolling onto my back, I smile up at him. He lies beside me, kissing my shoulder as he pulls me into his arms. Sinking my fingers into his jet black coils, I massage his scalp. He groans, making me smile.

"Your touch is medicine," he mutters.

"From not wanting to be near me to being your medicine."

He laughs jovially. "We were off to a rough start. But at least you're gorgeous. Blinds me to your annoying behaviors."

"Excuse me?!" I grab a fistful of his hair, playfully tugging it, and making him laugh harder.

"I said at least you're gorgeous because it blinds me to your – "

"I heard what you fucking said." His laugh is too infectious for me to not join him. "And the audacity of you to repeat it." I let go of his hair.

"Only joking, Snowflake." He smiles, bringing his lips to mine. "Tell me what you've been up to after you exiled me."

I roll my eyes, laughing. "You're getting a little too comfortable, Snow. I know good and damn well you heard Aspen say all I did was whine and complain. Something tells me you just want to hear how miserable I was without you."

"Maybe." The corner of his mouth tips up.

"Aspen's loudmouth already told you enough. Tell me what *you've* been up to."

He rolls onto his back, letting out a puff of air.

I prop myself up on my elbow. "That bad?"

"I would use the word freeing."

"Damn, better off without me?" I give him a look of incredulity.

"No." He smirks, meeting my gaze. "Believe me, I was miserable. Took a lot for me to not come here and invade your space. It was freeing because..." His voice trails off. I look at him expectantly, raising my brows. "Because Brielle helped me let go of Kenna's stuff, and I put the house on the market."

My jaw drops. "Really?"

He nods. "Yep."

I swallow, sitting up, and crossing my legs. "Snow... you didn't do this because of me, right? I truly meant what I said about taking your time."

Now I feel selfish for even bringing it up.

"You were an inspiration... well, more like a kick in the ass." I laugh. "But no, it had been a long time coming. I realized if I were to ever move on, with or without you, I can't do that clinging to the past. Everything in that house was a constant reminder of her and what we had."

Leaning forward, I wrap my arms around him. "I know that wasn't easy."

He hugs me back. "I don't think anything is ever truly easy."

I laugh softly, pulling away. "Yeah, true. How do you feel?"

"Like I severed the anchor to my past. After you left... I was back to being my miserable grinch self." I clap my hand over my mouth, trying not to laugh and fail. He smiles at me. "You light up my fucking world, Noelle. I don't want to take your light; I just want to bask in it by being in your space."

Tears prick my eyes, and I try to blink them away. I'm not successful as one trickles down my cheek. He swipes it away, giving me a look of concern.

"I know you don't think you're good with words, but you say the most beautiful things to me."

"Maybe I just had to meet you." He smiles.

"See." My eyes brim with tears. "If you hadn't noticed, I'm a crier."

"Believe me, I've noticed. I just wasn't going to give you shit about it."

I snort with laughter. "Generous of you."

"I try my best."

"Wait..." My eyes widen. "What are you going to do now that you're selling your house? Are you staying there until it sells."

"I can't." He shrugs. "It's not that there were never any good memories, but I only remember the bad there. It's not good for my mental health. North is letting me stay with him until I find a place."

I focus on one of the tattoos on his chest, tracing the lines of it with my fingertips. "You know... I mean–there's–well if you wanted to..." My voice trails off.

"I'm sorry. What language was that?" He quirks a brow with a grin.

I return his smile. "I just... you may think it's weird, but if you want to stay here, with me, you can. Maybe it's too soon and– "

"You want me to stay with you?"

"I know it's not as big as your place is and sometimes my neighbors are loud. You can also hear the train every night around midnight. And– "

"Noelle... that's not what I asked. Do you want me to stay with you?" Tilting his head to the side, he catches my gaze.

"Yes," I say without blinking. "You just feel... right to me, Snow. We're already inseparable. But only if you're comfortable."

"The question is are you comfortable? I've been living alone for a while. I remember you said you lived with your sister and then your ex. Did you want time to live by yourself to experience that?"

"Are you trying to talk me out of it?" I smile.

"No. I'm ready to go pick up my bags at North's place now." He points his thumb over his shoulder. "But I don't want you to feel like I'm invading your space."

The last time I lived alone was when I moved out at eighteen. Aspen graduated two years later, but stayed at home while she went to college to avoid getting a job. I was on my own for nearly four years before she asked to move in with me.

"You're not. I wouldn't have offered otherwise, but thank you for asking about my needs."

He gives me a confused look. "That's a pretty basic thing to do for someone you care about."

"Have you met the men these days? Because the bar is in hell."

He lets out a rumble of laughter. "Can't say I've dated a man, but I have a brother who emulates that sentiment."

"Eve seemed to humble him with a look."

"Yeah... she's always had that effect on him. They'll figure it out eventually."

It's apparent Eve is hurt, but when she wasn't glowering at Winter, she was looking at him with an intensity that you only see when two people are in love. I didn't know who he was, but when she would talk about him, it was clear she loved him deeply. Maybe they'll find their way back to each other.

"So... do you want to live with me or... ?"

He runs his hands down his face, letting out an exasperated sigh. "Do I want to live with the woman who pepper sprayed me?" I toss my head back, cackling. "The woman who thinks Moon Boots are fashionable? The very same woman who ran through the snow with her ass out and nearly caught hypothermia?"

"This isn't an opportunity to air your grievances," I say through laughter.

"Decisions, decisions." He clicks his tongue. "Live with the woman who annoys and captivates me in the same breath – "

"Fuck you."

"Or live with my brother? That's a tough one, Snowflake." He gives me a brilliant smile.

"You know what, I take back my offer. I don't – "

He has me on my back in a millisecond, silencing my words with his lips. "There's no place I'd rather be than right here with you."

17
SNOW

AFTER LINING UP MY beard, I stare at Noelle in the mirror as I rinse off my razor. We're getting ready side by side for friends and family night at Brielle and Ezra's brewery–Last Glass Brewery. Noelle is fixing her hair that's currently in faux locs down to her ass, in the mirror. She glances between me and her hair a few times, realizing I'm staring at her.

"What? Does my outfit look bad?" She's wearing black leather pants with a sheer white long sleeve top that has one button fastened below her breasts.

"No, stunning as always."

She grins. "Thank you. Go get your clothes on before *you* start something and we end up missing the event." Her eyes trail down the length of my body.

I stop behind her, grabbing her chin, and tilt her head to the side as I kiss her temple. "Wise choice." Smacking her ass, she yelps and laughs as I leave the bathroom.

The past couple of months with her have been surreal. I can't say I'm myself again because I don't remember who I was before the grief and loss. I'm re-discovering who I am with Noelle by my side. I was worried we happened too fast. That we'd crash and burn. But after moving in, and being in her space, I realized love doesn't give a fuck about time. It can break you, strip you down to nothing. But it also shows up when you need it. When you're ready. I'm not sure when I fell, but I dove into the depths of her headfirst and have zero intention of ever coming up for air. I just have to tell her.

After slipping on my shirt, I glance at myself in the mirror. Noelle has been filling my wardrobe with color. Would I have ever picked out a rustic burnt orange shirt myself? Absolutely not. But looking in the mirror, I have to admit, it's working for me.

Noelle appears, smiling. She smooths her hand over my chest. "I knew you'd look delectable in that color. Who knew having a boyfriend could be like having my own Ken doll?"

"Is that why you're with me? To dress me up?"

"It's a bonus." She kisses my cheek. "Are you ready?"

"Yeah." I slip my hand into hers as we walk out the door.

Last Glass Brewery is teeming with people, food, music, and of course, delicious beer. Brielle and Ezra have a gift for creating spaces for people to gather in.

"Will Eve be here?" Winter glances around.

"Uh... I don't know." I smirk. "Ask Noelle."

"No. It was just – " Before he can finish his sentence, she appears with Noelle and Aspen by her side.

"Looks like she will be here." North grins, looking at Winter.

"Yeah, I can fucking see that." He downs the rest of his beer.

"You may want to slow down so you don't make an ass of yourself," I suggest.

"Honestly, do you think I can go any lower than I already have?"

North and I laugh. "Have some fucking faith in yourself," I encourage him.

"I have faith she will have my head if given the opportunity," he mutters before they reach the table.

"Snow." Eve gives me a hug. "North." She gives him a hug too. Making sure the table is between her and Winter, she doesn't acknowledge his existence. I'm not sure if I should be concerned or laugh.

"Eve." Winter nods.

"Have you guys already ordered food?" Eve asks Noelle and Aspen, still ignoring him.

"Appetizers and beer," Aspen fills in.

"What if we ordered a couple of wood fired pizzas and wings?" Noelle suggests.

"As long as it doesn't have pineapple," North says, making a face.

Aspen gasps. "You don't like pineapple?"

"It doesn't belong on pizza."

"I beg to differ," Aspen retorts.

Noelle rolls her eyes. "Good luck debating her. She never shuts the fuck up. So pizza then?" She asks the rest of us as North and Aspen debate proper pizza toppings.

"That sounds good," Eve says.

"Yeah, it does," Winter chimes in.

Eve opens her mouth to say something, but I cut her off in an attempt to save Winter and our night. "Pizza and wings sound perfect."

We sort out toppings, pineapple being one of them to North's dismay, wing flavors, and drinks. Once our order is placed, Ezra and Brielle join us.

"Happy you're here." Ezra pulls me into a hug.

"Are you kidding? This brewery is amazing. I wouldn't miss it."

"You two are perfect together," Brielle says, looking between Noelle and me, beaming.

Draping my arm over Noelle's shoulders, I pull her into me and press a kiss to her temple. "We are."

She wraps her arms around my middle, looking up at me with the smile I've fallen in love with. We talk with Brielle and Ezra until they're called away by another table of friends. Our food arrives shortly after.

"When do you start back to school?" Eve asks Noelle.

"Spring." She smiles. "I'm looking forward to it."

Instead of getting another job, she enrolled in school to pursue her master's degree in library sciences. I'm so fucking proud of her and happy I get to encourage her along the way.

"Were you still thinking about getting a part time job?" Aspen asks.

"Uh... yeah." She tugs at her earring. I already know why she's uncomfortable. "I'm going to be helping Winter with marketing and social media at North Star Toys."

Eve chokes on her drink, coughing and sputtering. "What? You don't know anything about– "

"Neither did I," Winter cuts in. "She can learn and will be amazing."

"Why do you do that?" My brow furrows.

"Do what?" Winter asks, confused.

"Not you." I set my glass aside. "Eve." Noelle's eyes snap to mine with her lips slightly parted.

"What?" Eve wipes her mouth with a napkin.

"I've noticed you try to cut Noelle down whenever she does something you don't approve of, even if it makes her happy. So I'm curious as to why you do that?"

The table falls silent. Eve has done this multiple times now, and I've noticed Noelle always makes excuses. She's too nice. Luckily, I'm not.

"I – I..." Eve sputters.

I tilt my head to the side, waiting for her to find an adequate excuse, knowing there isn't one. Noelle isn't just nice, she's kind. I don't doubt Eve cares about Noelle. I know she loves her. But she's not going to use her as a doormat whenever she's feeling a certain way.

"I don't do that," she replies.

"Yeah, you do..." Noelle says softly, looking down at her hands. "Eve..." She quickly glances at Winter. "I don't know what happened between you and Winter, but that's something for the two of you to work out." She motions between them. "Not for you to take out on me. You said you're happy for me– "

"I am," she insists.

" –But I have yet to feel that from you," she finishes, meeting her gaze. "I plan to be with Snow until he gets tired of me." I chuckle, knowing that's never going to happen. "So figure it out, for the sake of our friendship."

For the first time tonight, Eve looks at Winter. They stare at each other before she tears her eyes away from him, looking at Noelle.

"I'm sorry."

"Thank you." Noelle smiles, her shoulders relaxing.

"You have permission to marry my sister."

"What the fuck?" Noelle gapes at Aspen.

She shrugs, taking a drink of her beer. "I'm just saying if it ever comes up, he has my vote."

Laughter ripples around the table as Noelle groans, covering her face with her hand. "Thanks... I guess."

The energy of the table shifts back to one of friendly conversation as we enjoy the good food. Brielle and Ezra take a moment to speak to everyone, thanking us for coming out and the plans they have for Last Glass Brewery. I'm grateful we reconnected on Mistletoe Mountain. Noelle was right, it's hard to show up for people when we can't even see ourselves, but I'm happy to witness this moment of their success.

As the crowd cheers with their final words, Noelle turns to me with a smile. "Want to get some fresh air?"

"Yeah."

"We'll be back." She hops off the barstool, pulling me along behind her. Making her way through the crowd, she heads toward Brielle and Ezra, giving them both hugs once she reaches them. "Congratulations, you two."

"Thank you," they reply with smiles.

"Are you leaving?" Ezra asks.

"No, getting some air," I reply.

"Oh, you should check out the balcony!" Brielle exclaims. "It's not open yet because I want to add some finishing touches. But," she points to a staircase, "if you take those stairs you'll have a better view of the fireworks we're about to set off."

"Giving us the presidential treatment." Noelle grins. More people are waiting to speak with Brielle and Ezra. "We'll let you get back to your guests. Thanks again," she says over her shoulder as we head for the stairs.

Once we're on the balcony, the noise of the party fades away, and it's just us looking out at the glinting lights of Hope Valley. After a few minutes of admiring the view, she turns to look at me.

"Thank you for saying something to Eve."

I smile, resting my hands on the railing on either side of her. "No one, not even your parents, will ever be allowed to talk to you that way."

Laughter tumbles from her lips. "Even my parents?"

"Parents, grandparents, great grandparents... anyone can get it when it comes to you, Snowflake."

She looks up at me with a glimmer in her eyes. "Why do you call me Snowflake? Or is it like the reason you let me stay in the cabin with you?"

"I wasn't going to lie to you. You're gorgeous and that was the reason I asked you to stay." She laughs, playfully pushing my arm.

"As for calling you Snowflake..." I take a step closer to her, cupping her chin. "It isn't because you ran naked in it." She smiles, brilliantly. "I call you Snowflake because each one is unique. No two are the same. You're mine. No one is you, nor will anyone ever compare." I press a soft kiss to her lips. "I love you, Snowflake."

Her brown eyes hold mine, lips slightly parted. "Love?"

"Yes, Noelle. Love. I love you, and I'll never grow tired of you."

Clasping her hands around the back of my neck, she smiles. "I love you too, Snow."

Fireworks light up the sky as I pull her flush against me, kissing her, knowing I'm holding the other half of me.

EPILOGUE
Snowflake

THE SETTING SUN BURNS on the horizon, making the cerulean ocean waves glitter. This breathtaking view should be enough to calm my nerves, but my knee bounces as I nibble on my lip.

Snow grabs my hand, pressing a kiss to my knuckles. "Nervous?"

Tearing my gaze away from the ocean zipping past us, I place my hand over my stomach that's tied itself in anxious knots. "I'm meeting your mom." I let out a sigh, resting my head against the car's seat. "That gives me every reason to be nervous. What if she doesn't like me?"

I'm looking forward to spending time with him and his mom, even if my excitement is clashing with my anxiety.

"I can't see how anyone couldn't like you. Unless you're armed with pepper spray..." He side eyes me with a smirk. I lean into him, laughing. "Do you have any on you now? Can't have you trying to take my mom out."

"Did you... tell her how we met?"

"That you assaulted me? Hell yeah, I did."

"Snow!" I swat his arm. "Why would you put it under those terms? *Assaulted*? Really?"

"Because it's true, Snowflake." He shrugs. "You'll also be delighted to know she laughed at me. Said I deserved it."

I snort with laughter. "I think we'll get along just fine then."

Talking to Carol is like catching up with an old friend. She's warm and inviting. It'd be impossible to feel uncomfortable around her. She has rich terracotta skin with zero wrinkles. The only clue to her age are the streaks of grey running through her sable colored curls. Snow favors her with the same deep brown eyes lined with dark lashes and full lips. We're sitting on the deck that overlooks the ocean, enjoying wine and conversation. Snow grabs the bottle, attempting to pour me another glass, but it's empty.

"There's more on the rack in the pantry, honey," Carol says.

Watching Snow with his mom warms my heart.

"Did you want more?" Snow tips the empty bottle toward me, raising a brow.

"I'm not going to say no to good wine." I smile.

"Coming right up." He stands, pressing a kiss to my temple before heading inside. I watch him, like I always do, still in awe we're together.

"You're head over heels," Carol says, pulling me from my thoughts.

I tear my eyes away from Snow as he disappears into the house, giving her a smile. "Irrefutably."

"Thank you for putting the light back in his eyes."

"As much as I'd like to take credit– " she chuckles " –Snow has done the necessary work for others to see the light he carries within himself again. It's always been there, just dimmed a little."

I still remember the first time I saw the flicker of light in the depths of his eyes. While it's flattering of her to presume I'm the reason, it discredits everything he's been through and the work he's done to be here with us, even though I know that's not her intention. Snow has made the effort, and I have the honor of being by his side.

"I feared I'd never see him happy again." She looks out at the waves. "It's hard to watch your child struggle, knowing there's nothing you can do to help them."

"Sometimes... we don't need help. We just need the space to feel what we feel, knowing there's someone in our corner."

She looks at me, tilting her head to the side. For a moment, she reminds me of Snow and the look he gives when he's not sure what to do with me. Maybe I said the wrong thing.

"Thank you." She smiles, calming my uncertainty. "I needed to hear that. My boys know without a doubt that I love them and am always here."

"And that's enough."

"Goodness, Noelle. You're a breath of fresh air." She pats my leg as Snow reappears with another bottle of wine. "I'm grateful you two have each other."

Sunlight peeks through the curtains as I lay in Snow's arms. It's a treat to wake up next to him and the sound of crashing waves.

"What did you want to do today?" he asks, pressing a kiss to my temple.

Stretching, I let out a sigh. "Anything. I don't care. I'm just happy to be here."

He chuckles. "We can go sailing again or we could do a picnic at that botanical garden with the bookstore that you were talking about."

I sit up, looking at him. "That's right! Books, a garden, *and* food? Honestly, what could be better?"

"Books, a garden, and food it is." He smiles. "Shall we have breakfast first?"

"Yeah, did you want to go somewhere or– "

He rolls on top of me and kisses his way to my center, settling between my thighs. "I meant you, Noelle. I want you for breakfast."

Looking down at him, I bite my lip. "Be my guest." Fisting the sheets, I inhale sharply as he tastes my center.

Snow watches me, holding a stack of books in his arms, as I look at *every* shelf in the bookstore. When I said I loved books, I don't think he realized it's an obsession. I grin at him as I set another book on top of the pile.

"I think that'll do."

"You sure?" He raises a brow. "I feel like I could hold– "

"If you insist." I place three more books on top of the stack.

" –More." He laughs.

"Oh," I clasp my hands together. "I need a few bookmarks."

"I'm sure they'll enhance your reading experience," he says sarcastically.

I narrow my eyes at him. "The right bookmark is like the cherry on top of a sundae."

Snow is painfully aware that I lose each and every bookmark I buy. He side eyes me before letting out a sigh as he waits for me to pick some out.

I choose a few with various sayings and pretty charms, placing them on top of the stack.

"I'm ready." I say for the hundredth time. He stares at me, waiting to see if I change my mind. "For real this time."

"Alright, Snowflake. Let's go."

Once my mountain of books are securely in the car, we head for the garden. We're surrounded by camelias, bonsais, orchids, and many more vibrant, lush plants. We settle on a patch of grass near the camelias. The scent of the roses is carried toward us by the warm breeze. Grabbing the picnic basket, I begin taking out the contents. Snow packed it and everything smells delicious.

"Did you make this?" I hold the carafe in my hand.

"Yeah. It's blackberry lavender lemonade. You're always amazed I can do basic things like... feed myself."

I laugh, shaking my head. "I'm not sure there's anything you'd do that I wouldn't find amazing."

He breathes and I'm enamored by it. Okay, that may be a little obsessive, but Snow treats me like the ground I walk on is blessed.

"I didn't make those." He says as I pull out the sandwiches. "Mom made them."

"That's sweet of her." I smile, taking out the container of fruit. "I've really enjoyed getting to know her. Thank you for bringing me here." Leaning forward, I press a kiss to his lips.

I pull out the rest of the items. Plates, napkins, dessert, and beneath it all is a book.

"Snow..." I smile. "Why is there a copy of The Grinch in here?" Opening the book, I gasp. The cover is The Grinch, but there are pages folded inside to form the words "Marry Me?", reminding me of a pop-up book.

My eyes meet his, and he's kneeling before me with a black velvet ring box in his hand. "Noelle Frost, you saw me when I couldn't see myself. I know in my heart, and with everything that I am, I am yours and you are mine. Will you marry me?" Opening the box, he reveals a glittering diamond ring in the shape of a snowflake.

I'm flooded with emotion, launching myself at him, wrapping my arms around his neck. "Yes. Yes. Yes." I repeat as we topple backward, landing chest to chest as I rain kisses on his face.

His laughter fills the air as he holds me. "Can I put the ring on you now?"

"Oh!" I sit up, straddling him. "I'm just so happy." Tears blur my vision.

Grabbing my hand, he slides the ring onto my finger, and presses a kiss to it. "Perfect."

I hold my hand up, watching the ring glint and gleam in the sun's rays. Meeting his gaze, I give him the biggest smile. "I love you so much, Snow."

"I love you too, Noelle. Looks like I can catch a snowflake after all."

Thank You

THANK YOU FOR READING. If you enjoyed this novel, please consider leaving a review on Amazon, Goodreads, and wherever else you can so other readers can enjoy it, too!

Keep in touch with me. Subscribe to my newsletter and follow me on social media to be the first to know about new releases, giveaways, freebies, and more!

Scan the QR code to listen to playlists, sign up for my newsletter, keep up with me on social media, and check out my other books.

Books by
A.E. Valdez

Made in the USA
Columbia, SC
02 September 2024

41423774R00126